IF I COULD DO IT AGAIN

IF I COULD DO IT AGAIN

ASHLEY STOYANOFF

ASHLEY STOYANOFF BOOKS
London, Ontario

Also by Ashley Stoyanoff

The Soul's Mark Series
The Soul's Mark: FOUND
Waking Dreams, A Soul's Mark Novella
The Soul's Mark: HUNTED
The Soul's Mark: BROKEN
The Soul's Mark: CHANGED

Deadly Trilogy
Deadly Crush
Deadly Mates
Deadly Pack

PRG Investigations Series
Two Truths and a Lie
Play It Again

Dedication

For Andrew.
Thank you for being you.

1

He's a Criminal

I don't know why I did it.

When I started writing the letter, I told myself that I was doing something good. I could be a friend to someone who needed it, a layer in his support system. But now that the letter is in the mail and I'm realizing just how much it can disrupt my life, I'm beginning to think there's probably a little more to it than that.

Maybe I'm bored, or perhaps it's because I need some excitement in my life. It could be because I'm lonely and I've been feeling that way for far too long. Or maybe, *just maybe*, I'm finally ready to take my life back, and sending out that letter was my first step.

Does that make me a horrible person?

I hope not, though I'm certain my husband will think so.

Husband ... what a joke. We may be legally married, but we haven't been *married* for quite some time. Sure, we still live together—when he's actually home—but I can't remember the last time we kissed, let alone had sex. We barely talk. Rarely see each other. The truth, we're more like roommates than spouses.

So why did I send that letter? All I really know for sure is that I need something ... more. I need to connect with someone and I really can't think of anyone who may understand the isolation or the trapped feeling that's eating away at me better than someone like Joshua. Someone who's stuck behind a prison fence.

I'm sitting in my office at my oversized oak desk, once more alone in my house. It's raining outside, the heavy drops splatting against my window. The blinds are open, and every few minutes I find myself looking out over the rectangular in-ground pool, watching the water dance as the rain falls. There's a mini river trucking around the travertine pool deck, seeping into the perfectly manicured flower beds. And just beyond our property I can barely make out a tugboat on the Atlantic Ocean making its way into the Halifax harbor. It's a beautiful view, perfect even with the rain. But God, I hate this house. I hate everything it represents. If it wasn't for this room—my office—I'd probably go insane here.

It's my sanctuary.

It's everything I dreamed of as a child.

Built-in floor to ceiling bookshelves covering two walls,

packed full with every genre of romantic fiction out there. There's even a sliding ladder like in the movies.

With a heavy sigh, I turn back to my laptop and reach for my electronic cigarette. The key to quitting smoking, I've found, is ensuring that the device is always fully charged. Well, that and using an e-liquid that tastes nothing like a real cigarette. Although, I haven't exactly quit smoking, so maybe my whole keys to quitting aren't really keys at all. The truth is, I probably smoke more now that I use the electronic cigarette than I had before, and if it weren't raining, I'd probably be sitting at the pool right now, puffing away on the real thing.

I take a deep pull from my electronic cigarette, tasting the sweetness of the caramel macchiato e-liquid as I stare at the blank *Word* document on my computer screen. It's taunting me, the cursor bar flashing at me. I haven't been able to write much these last few months, not since I told Richard that I don't love him anymore.

At least he's gone for a couple weeks this time. Maybe the space will help clear my head.

In all honesty, I probably should have left months ago, but fear holds me here. Fear of the unknown. Fear of starting over. Just thinking about it causes my chest to tighten and for a moment, just a brief second, I consider once again running out to the mailbox and standing there until the post lady comes. Maybe if I show identification, she'll let me retrieve the letter.

Probably not.

I take another drag from my electronic cigarette as I look at Joshua's profile once more, and then minimize it, focusing my attention on the fresh document.

Seconds pass ... five ... ten ... fifteen ...

My mind's blank. All my stories ... gone.

I puff away, taking drag after drag as I glare at the screen.

Setting the device down, I place my fingers on the keyboard. Another few seconds pass me by and I finally start to type. It comes slowly at first and it's random stuff, just thoughts and feelings. But at some point, what started as a journal style entry turns into something—something amazing. The minutes turn into hours and I get completely lost in my work.

It's exhilarating.

It's freedom.

It's ...

The front door slams. The sound startles me so much that I jump, yelping, and nearly fall off my chair. My heart races as I turn toward my closed office door, and I listen to the sound of someone banging around the house, opening and closing the fridge, slamming cupboard doors.

Swallowing a groan, I turn back to my computer. Guess I'm not alone anymore. I should have known Richard wouldn't stay gone for long. He never does, always popping back in with no warning. I just hope he isn't planning on staying too long this time.

He thumps up the stairs, but doesn't come into my office, doesn't bother to say *hi*, and moments later, I hear the door across the hall open and close and then I catch a whiff of glue fumes. *Crap.* He's working on his latest ship-in-a-bottle project. He's going to be here for the entire night, at the very least.

I linger in my office for a while, stalling, pretending to work as I pull up Joshua's profile once again, letting my eyes scan over his picture, wondering—again—what exactly I was thinking when I sent that letter. There's nothing overly friendly or inviting about him. His eyes are dark, brown or maybe black. It's hard to tell. His expression is closed-off and kind of hard, but he's hot even if it's in a scary kind of way. He's not smiling, flexing his impressive muscles. His hair is cut close, and he has a cleanly trimmed goatee. I can see some tattoos on his arms, but I can't quite make out what they are. If I passed him on the street, there's no way I'd have the guts to actually approach him.

Ugh. He's way out of my league, even for the friend zone.

Sighing, I lock my computer screen and sit back in my chair. The thought is eating away at me, bogging up my brain and weighing me down. I'm really not sure when I started thinking so poorly of myself, but I do know I don't like it. Not one bit.

I glance around my office, trying to clear my mind as I pick up my glass of water. It's warm now, despite it having been half full of ice when I first poured it. I take a sip anyway, savoring the way the liquid feels against my parched throat, before I finally stop stalling, and go find Richard.

He's sitting on the floor of his hobby room, bathed in the bright white lamp light, his fingers carefully holding a pair of long tweezers as he adds a piece of the ship through the slim bottle neck.

I step into the room, pausing beside him. Richard's attention doesn't shift from his project, though I can tell he knows I'm standing here. His jaw ticks and clenches, and he readjusts, turning away from me ever so slightly, shielding his precious ship from my view.

"You're home," I say, forcing a smile. "I thought you had to be in Calgary for a couple weeks this time."

"I do," he says.

Okay ... I stare at him, waiting for him to explain. He looks good, tired, but good, although the darkness under his eyes does make him look slightly older than his thirty-eight years. His white-blond hair is gelled and perfectly styled. His tie is loosened and the top few buttons of his shirt, undone. He's still dressed in his suit pants—the thousand-dollar suit is getting rumpled and dirty, the jacket tossed in a heap in the middle of the floor. Why isn't he sitting on the chair? Better yet, why didn't he change before he opened up the glue and paints? Guess I'll be making another trip to the drycleaners this week.

When he says nothing more, I ask, "Are you home long?"

"Not sure."

"Did the meeting get canceled?" I ask, feeling that all too familiar frustration creeping in, heating my face.

"No."

Brow creasing in annoyance, I turn to leave. Clearly he's not in the mood to fill me in and if I stay here any longer, I'll end up yelling at him. Seriously, why does he have to be so difficult?

As I start for the door, I consider mentioning the letter to Richard. I'm not sure why. It's really none of his business, but the thought crosses my mind anyway. Maybe it's because I want to see if he'll care. Or maybe it's because I've never hidden things from him before and now that he knows how I feel about him, there's no point in starting now. But whatever the reason, a part of me wants to keep Joshua to myself, sealed inside me where he's only mine.

I take another step toward the door, and then stall, something that feels a hell of a lot like guilt pausing my footsteps.

Right, okay, so I need to say something.

Damn guilt.

"By the way ..." I start, clearing my throat. "Remember that prisoner pen-pal website I told you about?"

"Yeah," he grunts, still not looking up from his project. God, I hate those damn ships. Hate the smell. Hate the way they look. Hate that they are more important to him than anything else in his life.

"Well, I sent a letter today," I say, slipping my arms around my waist.

He moves then, his head turning toward me, his eyes regarding me quickly from across the room, before settling his gaze back on the bottle. When he speaks, his voice is cold and dry. "You better be joking, Vic."

I blink at the sharp response, feeling a ripple of anger travel up my spine as heat settles into my cheeks. "No, I'm not joking. I told you I was going to, and well," I shrug, "I did."

"Huh." He looks at me then, really looks at me, his eyes a frosty blue. "So who is he? What did he do?"

"His name's Joshua Larson," I say, holding his angry gaze. "He killed someone in a bar fight. It was self-defense."

He laughs once, casting me a cynical look. "If it was self-defense, he wouldn't be in prison."

Right, okay, that was my first thought, too, but ...

The urge to defend this man, a man I've never met or even spoken to before, a man who enjoys beaches and has taken up beadwork, overwhelms me. I let my arms fall from my waist, planting them on my hips.

"He's a biker," I say oversensitively. "And he was wearing his club colors when it happened. I'm pretty sure if he wasn't, he wouldn't be where he is now."

"Huh," he says again. "A biker." He pauses, his cold eyes drawn back to the ship once again. A moment passes, and then another. I'm about to walk away, figuring the conversation's over, when he asks, "Where's he at?"

"He's in Pennsylvania and ..."

Richard cuts me off. "Jesus Christ, that's right across the border."

I roll my eyes. "It's not right across the border, it's like sixteen hours, one province, and five states away."

His expression hardens, his eyes darkening, and he gives me a look. It's a look that makes me tremble, a look that scares me. There's nothing loving about the look, nothing nice, and I find myself struggling not to back down, not to walk away.

He won't hurt me.

I know it.

The worst this man can—will—do to me is with his words.

It's always words with him, but they cut just as deeply as any knife could.

I glance around the room anxiously. I'm not sure what to say, or do, or even what to think. I wasn't really expecting this kind of reaction. I told him weeks ago about getting a pen-pal, and he seemed ... okay with it.

Actually, he didn't seem to give a shit what I did.

I just stare back at him and wait.

And wait.

And wait some more.

"You better not have given him our address," he says eventually.

I didn't, thinking it was safer to use my business post office box. After all, Joshua is a convicted criminal. Although I'm not about to tell Richard that.

"What does that matter?" I ask, hating how small my voice sounds. "He's in prison, and when he gets out he won't be permitted to cross the border."

"Don't be so goddamn naïve," he shouts, dropping the bottle. I hear a thump as it hits the ground. "He's a criminal, a goddamn gang member. If he wants to get into Canada, he'll figure it out."

"He's not a gang member," I shoot back at him instantly. "He's in a motorcycle club."

"Do you know how stupid you sound right now?" He glares at me for a long moment, and then shakes his head. "What makes you think he'd want to talk to someone like you anyway?"

"What's that supposed to mean?" I ask, though it's a rhetorical question. I already know what he's hinting at.

Slowly, his eyes scan me from the top of my head to the tip of my toes, before trailing back up again. A nasty little smirk turns upwards on his lips as he settles his gaze on my belly. "How's that diet of yours going, Vic?"

"You're an asshole," I say, fighting against the urge to fold my arms around my midsection once more.

"Maybe." He shrugs. "But I'm good to you. I don't hit you. I've got a multimillion dollar job and pay all the bills while you play at your writing. You could have done a lot worse."

Maybe, but sometimes I really wonder if being poor and dealing with physical abuse would have been better than the emotional turmoil this man puts me through.

"I've got work to do," I mutter, not at all surprised when he says nothing, grabbing his bottle and inspecting the ship for damage.

Tears leak from the corner of my eyes as I turn to leave. I go straight to my office, shutting the door and leaning up against it, groaning when I catch sight of my reflection in the mirrored closet doors.

I look awful.

My eyes are bloodshot, tears streaking down my cheeks. My hair is neatly pulled back, twisted into a bun, sitting high on my head, making my face look thick and puffy, and I'm wearing a tank top and yoga pants.

Oh God. My outfit hides nothing.

Grimacing, I straighten up, stepping closer to the mirror. I suck in my belly, roll my shoulders back, and lift my chin. I've come a long way over these last six months, losing twenty-seven and a half pounds, but at this moment I can't see it.

All I see is fat.

A sagging bulge under my chin, love handles, and a rounded belly. Turning to the side, I take in the lumps at my bra line, big ass, and thick thighs. There's fat everywhere. I've always had big hips and a generous backside, but what happened to my size eight body?

I push and prod, adjusting my stance, trying to minimize the problem areas, but no matter how I stand, how I hold myself, the lumps and bulges still show through, and the damn tears keep falling.

Maybe Richard's question holds merit. Why would Joshua want to talk to someone like me?

Stepping away from the mirror, I snag my electronic cigarette off of my desk and a book off the shelf, and then I curl up in my big bowl chair and I wrap myself in a blanket. I don't actually open the book, just hold it, seeking comfort from the feel of the pages within my hands.

Hours or minutes or seconds. I don't know how long it takes before the tears finally stop, but the moment they do exhaustion hits, and sleep pulls me away.

And then, I'm roused awake.

My office is dark, the house, silent, and my mouth is so dry it feels like sandpaper scratching down my throat each time I swallow. Sliding out of my chair, I slip out of my office and pad down the stairs. As I head for the kitchen, I notice that Richard's shoes are gone from the front door and his wallet and keys are missing from the counter.

I pour myself a glass of water, before making my way through the house and glancing out the front window, confirming that his car is in fact gone.

I smile. He's not here anymore.

I wander between rooms for a bit, making sure that all his things are gone, that there's no chance he'll be showing back up in an hour or two, before I make my way to my bedroom. I wrap myself up in the blankets, and cuddle up to the pillows, closing my eyes.

When I drift off again, I sleep deeply.

2

Letters

It's been nearly two weeks since I sent the letter to Joshua, and I'm starting to think he's not going to write me back, but that doesn't stop me from getting into my car and going to the post office every day at three-thirty on the dot to check my post box.

Heading right into the post office, I bypass the counter, going straight for my box. As soon as I open it, instant disappointment settles over me.

It's empty again.

Closing the door, I lock it up and turn to leave when Grace calls out, "Hold on a second, Vickie. There's still more here. I haven't had a chance to sort through it all."

Those words stall me and my stomach does a little flip-flop. I smile at her. "Oh, sure, thanks."

Walking over to the counter, I lean against it, watching as she quickly flips through the stack of mail. She's a sweet lady, maybe ten years my senior, with long black hair and a bubbly voice. It takes a few minutes before she turns to me, a letter in her hand.

"Here you go," she says, smiling sweetly, setting the letter down on the counter. "I hope it's the one you've been waiting for."

My eyes widen as I stare at the large red stamp on the front of the envelope. *This letter has been mailed from the Pennsylvania Prison System.*

Oh my God. He wrote back.

I'm stunned. For a moment, all I can do is stare at the envelope, reading the stamp once, twice, three times, before glancing back at Grace, my hands shaking ever so slightly, itching to snatch it up, as excitement sparks throughout my entire body. She's eyeing me curiously, like she's hoping that maybe this really is the letter I've been waiting for.

I grin at her, grabbing the letter to leave. "It is. Thanks so much for checking for me."

"No worries, hon," she says. "See you tomorrow."

"See you." I stick the letter into my purse, feeling slightly dazed as I make my way out to my car. When I reach my house, I'm itching to tear it open. I head straight to my office and sit down at my desk, carefully opening it.

July 17, 2015

Hey Victoria,

What's good? I'm just chilling, listening to old school jams. I just got your letter this morning, and I'm really excited to get to know you better.

So you're a romance author. That's cool. I'm a hopeless romantic. I'd like to read your newest book if you want to send me a copy. No pressure. If you don't want to, I'll understand. I've never met an author before. What made you decide to write to someone like me? I'm really excited that you did.

You said that you're fiercely loyal. Great quality to have. I'm very loyal, too. Your word is all you have in life.

Good to know family is important to you. Family is everything to me. I'm the youngest of five kids. Grew up in Pennsylvania. I'm really close with my family. Do you have any siblings?

Could you send me a picture of you so I know who I'm talking to?

I'm really excited to get to know you better, so tell me a little bit more about yourself. Here are some questions for us to get to know each other better.

What is your sexiest feature?

What are three qualities that are important to you in the man you're dating?

What's your favorite color?

Are you dating anyone now?

Do you have any tattoos? If yes, what and where?

When's your birthday?

Describe your perfect first date.

If you could be anywhere in the world right now, where would you be?

Do you prefer sunrise or sunset?

What's one thing a person can do to make you fall in love with them?

Well, I'm going to cut this off here. Thank you for taking the time to write me. I hope you have a great week and I hope to hear back from you soon.

Your friend,
Joshua

P.S. I'm an open book so feel free to ask me anything.

I fold the letter carefully, setting it down on my desk and staring at it for a beat. He wants to get to know me. *Me.* And he wants a picture.

Shit.

My heart is pumping hard in my chest as I snag up my phone and quickly snap a few tester photos. I've never been much of a selfie taker, and it turns out it really isn't as easy as it looks.

Oh my God, do I have three chins?

Shit. Shit. Shit.

These pictures look ... awful. No, scratch that. They're way worse than awful.

Turning to my computer, I pull up Google, quickly

searching 'How to take a flattering selfie', and then I scan through the results, soaking up every tip and trick the internet has to offer me.

Two hours later, my hair is done, so is my makeup, and I'm back in my office. The curtains are open (supposedly natural light helps with the whole selfie taking thing) and I start taking pictures.

I take at least a hundred photos before I manage to get one that I kind of like. I consider editing and altering it for about half a second, but then decide not to. What's the point of having a pen-pal if I can't be one-hundred percent real with him?

So I print off the picture, open a *Word* document, and start typing ...

July 24, 2015

Hey Joshua,

How are you? It's good to hear from you. I've enclosed a picture of myself as requested. I hope you like it. *smiles*

Okay, to answer your question on why I decided to write to someone like you ... The truth is, it happened by accident. I was researching a book and stumbled upon the pen-pal site. Then I found your profile, and after a lot of research on you, I thought I'd take the chance and write you a letter.

You also asked if I'm dating anyone and I'm going to take a shot at explaining that, so bear with me because it's complicated.

The simple answer is yes, I am. Actually, I've been married for a little over two years now and I still live with my husband, but it's been over for some time now. If I'm being honest with myself, it was over before we said 'I Do', but I guess we all make mistakes.

He's quite a bit older than me, fourteen years to be exact. He's a successful tech consultant and when we met, I was a waitress. He used to come in and sit in my section whenever he was in town and flirt with me. I don't know if it was the expensive suits or his confidence or perhaps it was that he was handsome, but we started dating, and then two years ago, we got married.

Anyway, I've told him it's over, that I don't love him anymore, but he asked me to stay. He wants to try to work things out, and I guess I feel like I owe him that, but the thing is, there's just nothing left to work out. I just don't love him anymore. Actually, I'm not sure if I ever did.

I hope you don't think I'm a horrible person now. Sometimes I feel like I am, but the thing is, I really don't think he loves me either. I think he's just scared of change and what we have is comfortable for him.

Does that make sense? I hope so.

I'd be happy to send you one of my books. I'll package one up and send it out at the same time as this letter, so keep an eye out for it. I hope it gets to you okay.

Okay, I'm going to try to answer all of your get-to-know-you questions now. *smiles*

What is your sexiest feature? Hummm ... Well, I've been told I have bedroom eyes, so I think I'll go with that.

What's your favorite color? Purple!

What are three qualities that are important to you in the man you're dating? Easy. Honesty, nonjudgmental, and understanding.

Do you have any tattoos? If yes, what and where? I have three tattoos. One is a heart shaped key with a pink ribbon that says 'follow your heart' along the length of the key. That one is on my ribs along my right side. I have a hummingbird at the nape of my neck, and I also have an apple blossom tattoo stemming up from the center of my breast and curving along the left side of my collarbone. What about you? I noticed you had some tattoos in your picture. Tell me about them.

When's your birthday? It's February 19, 1991.

Describe your perfect first date. Let's see ... my perfect first date would be something simple, like a picnic on the beach.

If you could be anywhere in the world right now, where would you be? Oh, this one's easy. I'd be in Cuba. I love it there. They have some of the best beaches in the world and the people are so nice.

*Do you prefer sunrise or sunset? Both. I can't pick just one. *smiles**

What's one thing a person can do to make you fall in love with them? Wow, this one is really hard. I'm not sure if there is any one thing someone could do to make me fall in love with them. There's either a spark or there's not, and if it's not there, well, it's just not there. Does that make sense? I hope so.

Okay, I'm pretty sure I answered all your questions. Your turn ... I'm looking forward to reading all of your answers.

Well, I guess I better get back to work. Until next time ...

Hugs,
Victoria

It's easier to mail the letter this time. I barely hesitate as I stick it in the envelope along with the picture and head back to the post office. Actually, I'm almost ... excited. Excited to get to know this man. I hope he writes back again.

Days pass.

Long, drawn out days of nothing.

I spend most of my time writing, although I also agonize a fair bit. What if Richard is right? What if Joshua saw my picture and decided I wasn't worth talking to? What if I am too curvy and he doesn't want to be friends with someone like me?

It's crazy, I know. I'm crazy. But this waiting ... It's driving me insane.

When the next letter finally arrives, I'm buzzing with nerves and excitement.

August 8, 2015

Hey beautiful,

What's good? I'm just chilling. Just got back from REC. Worked on biceps and triceps today. I got your letter and picture.

You're beautiful, and those eyes, I could stare into them forever. And it looks like you have some nice big breasts, too.

I like how you put your smiles in the last letter. It's so fucking cute.

What are you thinking right now? I like to ask this question. It gives me a better idea of who you are and what you're about.

Have you ever listened to that Nicki Minaj song 'Hey Mama'? I'm listening to it right now. I think it's so fucking sexy. It's all about a woman taking care of her man. Very sexy. Very good song. You should listen to it.

I'm really excited to get to know you. I loved all your answers. Feel free to ask me anything you want. I'm an open book.

My sexiest feature is my smile, I think. I'm told I have a really great smile. I have five tattoos, two devils, one covering my chest and one on my left forearm. I got them because my family used to call me a devil child when I was a kid. I also have a tribal tattoo on my right bicep. I hate that one, but it's so big there's nothing I can do about it. It was one of my first. I've got two dragons coming together on my right forearm; that one means 'brother'. Me and another guy from the club got it together when I joined. And the last one is the one-eight-seven on my left ribs with my life story within the numbers.

I like that you have tattoos. So sexy on women.

Thank you for being so honest with me about your marriage. Honesty is really important to me, and I'm glad you told me the truth. I'm not dating anyone right now. I just broke up with this psycho bitch. She was a total head case, threatening me and my family.

Three qualities that are important to me in someone I'm dating would be honesty, loyalty, and caring, and one thing a person could do to make me fall in love with them would be to love me for me and not try to change me. Every woman I've ever dated has tried to change me. I fucking hate it. I'm open and very blunt so those bitches all knew who I was when we hooked up. I'm not going to change who I am for anyone. Words are the way to my heart.

My perfect first date would be a long ride on my motorcycle, then a nice dinner on the beach. I love the beach. The water calms me.

I'm a sunset kind of man, my favorite color is blue, and if I could be anywhere in the world right now, I'd be with my family. I miss them a lot and feel real bad for what I've put them through.

I hope you don't mind, but I have this question book I use when I write letters. It has thousands of questions to ask to get to know people better. Most of them are questions that we wouldn't normally think to ask. If you don't want me to use the book, just let me know. I just want to be one-hundred percent honest with you.

So tell me something new about yourself. Something new about me would be that I trained in martial arts since I was young. I really enjoyed it, and was really good. I can't wait to start again when I hit the streets.

Here are some more questions for you.

What gifts from your man mean the most to you?

What is the best thing about starting a new relationship?

What about love makes you afraid?

What do you see from your bedroom window?
Do you wear makeup all the time or only sometimes?
Have you had a recurring dream throughout your life?
What are your turn-ons and turn-offs?
Do you believe soul mates meet by accident or is it destiny?
Well, my beautiful girl, I've got to go. I hope you have an amazing week. I can't wait until your next letter.

Your friend,
Joshua

P.S. I made you something and you should have it soon. Hope you like it.

I'm smiling so big when I put the letter down that my cheeks hurt. He thinks I'm beautiful.

Me.

Beautiful.

And he made me something.

Surprised laughter escapes me. I should probably be worried about the more than friendly tone of the letter, but somehow I feel special and a little lighter than I have in years.

I feel ... giddy. Giddy and curious.

Who is this man?

3

Beads, Bracelets, and Dicks

―――――

"You've got two today, hon."

I smile widely at Grace's confirmation, feeling a blush overtaking my face as I rush over to my post box. My heart's racing as I unlock it and spot two letters, both from Joshua.

Quickly, I retrieve my mail and wave a quick goodbye to Grace as I head outside, nearly jogging to my car. I barely have the car door shut before I tear into the first one, pulling out a piece of folded tissue paper that's held closed with a sticker that reads, *Packaged with Love.*

My grin widens, and my cheeks begin to sting something that feels a hell of a lot like butterflies begin to dance in my belly. But it can't be butterflies, right? And

――

my heart is only thumping harder, pumping and skipping, because I jogged to my car, right?

It's not excitement.

It can't be nerves.

Shit. Who am I kidding? I'm excited. I'm nervous. I'm … I'm … floating, hovering on a wave and I'm pretty sure I'd be happy if it never crashes into the shoreline, letting me ride it forever.

Carefully, I peel the sticker off, unwrapping the paper and finding a bracelet within.

The bracelet is beautiful, handmade with these tiny purple beads. And oh my God, my name is woven along the front in white with two hearts, one on each side.

I don't know how to react as I sit here in my car, my eyes stinging slightly as they start to water and those butterflies in my belly take flight, flapping and fluttering, filling my entire body.

It's … perfect.

I've never had a man hand make jewelry for me before.

I can't believe Joshua actually made it.

When he wrote that he had taken up beadwork in his profile, I'd never truly believed it. It's kind of hard to picture this big, scary looking man working with tiny beads, but my God, it's amazing.

Abso-freakin'-lutely perfect.

I pick it up and set the envelope and tissue paper aside. Wrapping it around my wrist, it's easy for me to fasten it in place. It looks perfect there, better than perfect. I don't think I'll ever take it off.

Smiling, I stare at it for a second, five, ten, before curiosity gets the best of me. I open the other envelope and pull out a new letter.

August 11, 2015

How's my beautiful angel doing? I was so excited to get your letter today. I've been thinking about you all day, every day. Did you get the present I made you? I hope you like it. I'm glad you said in your last letter that you like handmade things, because that's really all I can do for you in here.

I got the book you sent today, too. I can't wait to start it. I'm going to start reading right after I finish this letter. Thank you from the bottom of my heart. It means so much to me. I can't believe you signed it to me. Means the world to me, beautiful. I'll treasure it always.

I'm just chilling now. Got back from REC not long ago. Worked on legs today. Do you work out? I work out six days a week, even when I was on the streets. It's a passion of mine. I used to compete in powerlifting growing up, before I hurt my back.

We had burgers today. That was cool. Most of the food is not so good here, but I like the burgers. We're going to have strawberry waffles this weekend. I'm really excited for that because I haven't had strawberries since I came to this prison. What's your favorite food?

Can I call you sometime? No pressure. If you're not ready, I'll understand. I'd just like to hear your voice is all. Think about it, and when you're ready let me know.

So what are you thinking about? I'm thinking about you, and about reading your book. The cover looks very sexy. I'm really excited to start it.

I enjoyed reading your answers to my questions. I think we have a lot in common. I really like that you're being one-hundred percent open with me. Here are my answers.

The best gift my girl could give me is her heart, and the best thing about starting a new relationship is the excitement of getting to know someone's likes and dislikes.

I'm definitely scared of being vulnerable and getting hurt when it comes to falling in love. If you give yourself to somebody and get hurt, it's like you did it for no reason.

From my bedroom window, I can see the grass, some birds, a basketball court, barbed wire fences, and farm fields behind that. It's so cool that you can see the ocean from your window. Could you send me a picture? I love the ocean and would really like to see what you see.

I get nightmares, too. They're really bad and I take sleeping meds because of them. I've been taking them for years and can't sleep without them.

My turn-offs would definitely be bitchy women. I can't stand women who bitch and moan all the time. As for turn-ons, big asses do it for me. I like thick thighs, too. Hair, makeup, and nails done. High heels are very sexy. And a woman that's caring and thoughtful is a huge turn-on.

As for soul mates, I believe we meet by destiny. I think there is someone out there for everyone and our whole lives lead up to finding that one person we're meant to fall in love with.

Tell me, what person in your life is the best example of love? How often have you fallen in love? What is the nicest thing you ever did for someone else? Define intimacy in your own words.

The question book I've been using also has a whole bunch of sexual questions in it, but I'm skipping them for you. I want to be respectful of your situation. Even if you don't love your husband, I don't want to come in between you two. So if I ask anything that bothers you or crosses the line, just let me know. Sometimes it's hard for me to know because I'm really open about sex with my friends. I want you to feel one-hundred percent comfortable with me all the time.

Well, gorgeous, it's time to eat and then I'm going to start reading your book, so I'm going to end this one here. I hope you have an amazing week and I'm really looking forward to your next letter. Hope you write back soon.

Sending you my love,
Joshua

P.S. I just got some new pictures of me. My parents are copying them and once I get them back I'll send you copies. They're also sending some pictures of my motorcycle so I can send them to you. Hope you like them.

It takes only a few minutes for me to get home after reading the letter. It's late afternoon, and the house looks quiet, though Richard's car is now parked in the driveway. I park beside him, strolling up to the house, pausing to stare at our perfectly manicured, oversized lawn, seeing the pool peeking out past the corner of our Greek Revival mansion. I shake my head. The house may be overly large and gorgeous, but it isn't worth my happiness. I'm not sure why I ever thought it was.

On the pillared entryway, I stop to pick up a box. I glance at the label, and grin a little. The swag I ordered for my next book launch has finally arrived.

Carrying the box inside, I smile politely to my neighbors as they wave hello. When I unlock the front door, juggling the box as I come in, Richard is standing in the foyer, arms folded over his chest. His expression is blank. He looks at me, his eyes shifting to the box in my arms, before he meets my eyes again. He's quiet for a moment, just staring at me, before he speaks, "Where have you been?"

"I went to check my mail," I say, closing the door and locking it. "When did you get back?"

He shrugs one shoulder. "About twenty minutes ago."

Twenty minutes ago? Was I really gone that long? *Huh.*

Walking through the house, I step into the kitchen, setting the box and my purse down on the countertop, before grabbing a glass from the cupboard and filling it with water from the fridge. Richard follows me, so closely I can nearly feel his hot breath puffing against the nape of my neck. He's agitated. I can feel it. The air around us is so thick it's suffocating and all I want to do is disappear into my office, except I know doing that will only make things worse.

"What's that?" he asks after a long moment.

"What?" I put the Brita jug away and close the fridge, before glancing at him.

"On your wrist," he says, his eyes narrowing as he stares at the beautiful beaded bracelet. "What the fuck is that on your wrist?"

I swallow hard, trying not to flinch at his sharp tone. I'm still on a high, my heart still racing from Joshua's letter and gift, and I don't want to let the feeling go.

Actually, I'd be happy if I could hold on to this feeling forever.

I pad over to the table, setting my glass down and taking a seat. "It's a bracelet." I place my elbows on the tabletop, folding my hands together in front of me.

Richard turns up his nose. "When did you have time to make a bracelet? You were supposed to be writing. Wasn't that the deal when I let you leave that waitressing job?"

"I didn't make it, Joshua did," I say, rolling my eyes and biting my tongue on the '*Fuck off*' that's trying to fight its way out of my mouth. I quit waitressing because Richard was worried about how it would look if his wife was working at a bar. It had nothing to do with my writing and everything to do with his image. The man has never supported my career choice, always treating it like a hobby. If he only realized how much I actually make ...

Richard laughs once, unamused. "It looks cheap."

"It looks perfect," I snap instantaneously.

He jerks back a little, as though my sharp response was a physical slap, and stares at me with wide eyes.

And there goes the high.

Silence falls.

Seconds pass, turning into minutes.

I sip my water, not sure what else to say.

Richard paces for a moment, before planting himself down on the chair across from me. He's still watching me, and I'm not sure what it is I'm seeing there in his eyes. Anger? Fear? A mix of both or something entirely different?

I have no idea.

His emotions are moving across his face so quickly that I can't track them or make any sense of them.

Finally, he speaks, keeping his voice low. "I know his kind."

I shift on my chair, turning slightly to face him as I take a sip of water. "And what *kind* exactly would that be?"

"He's a criminal," he says, leaning forward and resting his elbow on the tabletop. "He's playing you, preying on your low self-esteem. If he hasn't asked you for money yet, I bet he will soon. All it takes is one internet search to find out we're loaded. He doesn't give a shit about you, and the bracelet ... it's just all part of his fucked up game."

I wince. The idea that Joshua has been playing me has crossed my mind, so much so that I spent hours on Google looking into pen-pal relationships. I found some interesting articles, even one from an ex-convict pointing out what to look for. According to that one, Joshua, if anything, has been genuine so far. "Maybe you're right, but you could be wrong, too."

"I know I'm right," Richard says, his eyes suddenly heavy and tired, his age showing through. "This isn't one of your romance novels where the big, bad biker really has a heart of gold, Vic. He's not going to change into your knight in shining armor and save you from your *so-called* shitty life. You shouldn't believe all that shit you read. Life isn't like that. You've got to stop romanticizing this shit."

Romanticizing this shit? Huh. "I think life can be like that, and you know what, *Dick*, I'm not the only one that wants to believe it." My voice rises with every word, and I pause for a second, taking a calming breath, before continuing. "If I were the only one, romance books wouldn't be one of the top selling genres out there. And honestly, I don't even know why we're talking about this. He's just a pen-pal, a friend maybe. We've just started writing."

"I'm just saying, four years from now when he gets out, you'll still be stuck right here with me, and he'll be out doing whatever it is bikers do. There's no future for you with him. You're wasting your time."

His words make me shiver, because I think there may be some truth to them. Four years from now I may actually still be *stuck* here with him.

"He wants to talk on the phone," I mumble. "I'm going to look into that and try to set it up."

"No."

"No?" I ask, surprised.

"No," he repeats immediately. "You're not talking to that dirt bag on the phone."

I laugh, shocked. "You really don't have a say in this."

"You're living in my house, of course I have a say in it."

"It's our house, *Dick*. Ours, not yours." And it is. I may not have purchased it, but we're married. We don't have a prenuptial agreement—Richard didn't want one. Everything we have is fifty percent mine and that was his choice.

"Wow." He laughs once in disbelief, shaking his head. "You're still my wife, Vic."

"Maybe on paper." I close my eyes tight, letting out a deep breath before reopening them. "But I haven't been your wife for at least a year now and you know it."

"I get that you don't love me anymore," he says, keeping his voice low as though trying really hard not to yell, "but you promised you'd give me a chance to fix this. I've wasted two years of my life on you. You owe me."

I freeze for a moment, feeling like a cornered animal. *You owe me.* Do I? He's said it so many times since we met, each and every time he helped me with something. New car ... *you owe me.* Dinner ... *you owe me.* Officially moving me into his house ... *you owe me. You owe me ... You owe ...*

Shit. It's emotionally exhausting.

I sigh. "When are you going back to work?"

"Don't worry, sweetheart," he says, his tone full of disgust. "I'll be gone once my laundry is done."

4

Phone Calls

It takes me three weeks, three long, frustrating weeks to get the phone accounts set up.

When I decided to do it, I figured it would be easy. Something as simple as giving Joshua my number. As it turns out, nothing is easy when it comes to dealing with the prison system. I had to get a U.S. number because inmates in Pennsylvania aren't allowed to call outside the country, and then I had to set-up a prepaid calling account for collect calls and register my number.

Sounds pretty simple, right? Well, trust me, it's not. I've never had to jump through so many hoops in my life.

But even frustrating, these last three weeks have still been ... amazing. My world has been wrapped up in letters. Sweet, sweet letters from a killer.

Okay, maybe Richard is right. Maybe I am romanticizing things, but I don't care. The truth is, I've never been this freakin' happy.

Never.

And any day now, Joshua will be receiving the letter with my new Pennsylvania number.

It's sunny this afternoon, and Richard is home. It's Saturday, and as far as I can tell he's home for the weekend. I'm sitting on the couch with my laptop, trying to get a handle on my emails and clean up my inbox, when he thumps down the stairs.

"You want to go out?" he asks, pausing in the living room entryway. "I feel like getting some lunch, maybe taking a drive down to Peggy's Cove."

I shake my head quickly, keeping my eyes on my emails. "I'm just going to make something here and work."

"Come on, Vic. It's the weekend and I haven't been home in a month."

Pulling my gaze away from my laptop, I glance up at him. He's dressed in jeans today and his neatly pressed button up blue and green striped shirt is untucked with the top three buttons open. He's watching me, his expression almost pleading, as he takes a couple steps toward me. It's the same look he gave me the day I finally gave in and went on a date with him nearly three years ago. He was so persistent back then, asking me out every single time he came into the pub I worked at. I'd waited months to go out with him, because he was intimidating to me. So sure of himself, so ... impressively confident, and I could never understand why he wanted a waitress like me.

I still don't.

"Please, Vic," he says when I say nothing. "Spend some time with me. You promised you'd try."

"Yeah, okay," I mutter eventually, because he's right. I promised I'd try, though at this moment, I have no idea why I made such an absurd promise. "Lunch and then right back here. I really do have to work today."

Grinning, Richard turns away. "I'll meet you in the car," he says as he walks toward the front door. "Don't take long."

Pressing my fingers to my closed eyes, I let out a groan of frustration. I need to write the back cover story for my current work in progress and book a cover reveal tour. That's what I'd planned on doing today, but he sounded so sincere, like he really wants to spend time with me ...

Ugh ... When did I become so gullible?

Setting my computer down on the coffee table, I get up and make my way upstairs to change. Discarding my yoga pants and tee, I slip on my favorite sunflower printed baby-blue summer dress and a cute pair of ankle laced sandals. I let my hair down, running my fingers through it a few times. It's wavy from being tied up all day, but I don't have time to fix it, so I quickly pull it back up, twisting it into a French knot. I swipe some gloss onto my lips, and quickly put on some eyeliner and shadow, before rushing back downstairs and venturing out of the house.

I find Richard sitting in his Lamborghini Elemento, fiddling with the radio. God, I think that car is ugly, but I get in anyway and he speeds off to Starbucks, pulling into the drive-thru. He orders me a large coffee, with one milk and one sugar, surprising me when he remembers what I like—he never remembers—and he orders a black coffee for himself. He pays, handing me my drink, and then he starts driving once more, heading toward Peggy's Cove.

The conversation is strained at best. I try filling the silence with random chit-chat, but he pretty much shuts me down on every topic, only supplying small grunts or one-word responses, and after about ten minutes, I give up, staring out the window instead.

Minutes pass. The silence is nice, peaceful, and the view, beautiful, and I—surprisingly—find myself enjoying the drive.

And then my phone rings, shattering the quiet moment.

Digging my phone out of my purse, I glance at the caller display, seeing a Pennsylvania number flashing on the screen. My heart races and my stomach clenches tight. *It's Joshua.* I stare at the phone for a beat. Now that he's calling, I'm not sure I'm truly ready to talk to him.

"Who is it?" Richard asks.

His voice startles me, and I jump a little in my seat. *Shit.* I totally forgot about him. I shake my head quickly. "I think it's Joshua."

Richard frowns, cutting me a sideways look. "Answer it."

My face flushes. I really, really don't want to talk to him in front of Richard. "No, it's fine. I'm sure he'll call back later."

"Really, I don't mind. Take the call, Vic."

"No," I say again, this time louder. "I don't want to talk to him for the first time with you sitting beside me. It's kind of uncomfortable."

He laughs once, a dry, bitter sound that makes my stomach clench—hard. "Yeah, I guess talking to your new boyfriend in front of your husband would be awkward."

My face burns hotter, the heat, spreading down my neck, and I scoff. "Don't be ridiculous. He's just a friend."

The ringing stops and silence falls.

Five, ten, fifteen seconds pass.

My phone chimes, indicating a new voicemail.

"If he's just a friend," Richard says, "you would have answered it."

I'm not really sure what to say to that, so I merely lift a shoulder in a one-sided shrug, and slip my phone back into my purse.

And then, it rings again.

"He's calling again?" Richard asks.

I pull it back out and look at the screen, seeing the same Pennsylvania number flash there, and I shrug. "I guess so."

Richard's eyes narrow as he watches me silence the call. "Just answer it and tell him you're busy."

I don't answer it. Instead, I turn off the ringer, and put my phone back into my purse. Retrieving my electronic cigarette, I settle back into the seat, taking a drag and then a long sip from my coffee. I really freakin' hope he tries again later.

Eventually, we arrive at the restaurant, though Richard takes his time about it, turning the typical forty-five-minute drive into an hour and a half. The hostess seats us at a window table that offers a perfect view of the lighthouse. We order and we eat, though we scarcely talk, and by the time we finish our lunch I'm dying to get back home, wishing I'd never agreed to go out in the first place.

The drive home is just as strained as lunch, the conversation, minimal. As soon as we get there, I go to my office, shutting the door and opening the curtains. The sun is still shining, and the natural light feels warm against my skin as it beats through the window. I sit down at my desk, turning the ringer on my phone back on, and then open up my current work in progress with the intention of getting ahead on it. I end up abandoning it, though, curling up in my chair with a book when I realize I'm not getting anywhere.

And then ... I fall asleep.

I'm awakened much later by my phone ringing. My office is cloaked in darkness, a soft glow creeping in from under the door. Reaching for my phone, I pick it up and glance at the screen.

Joshua.

My heart stalls, and then races. I answer it tentatively. "Hello?"

I'm greeted with a recording, advising me that an inmate is calling, and informing me that all calls are recorded and monitored. I'm shaky, and jittery, waiting for the long drawn-out message to end. Finally, I'm prompted to accept the call. My finger is trembling with an equal mix of nerves and excitement as I pull the phone from my ear and I press the button. There's a pause of silence and then another recording advising that the call is being connected and it feels as though it drags on forever, before his voice finally breaks through. "Hey, beautiful. What's good?"

His voice isn't deep, but it isn't high either and he's speaking fast, the words slurring together. He sounds ... excited? Yeah, I'm pretty sure that's excitement I'm hearing in his voice.

I'm grinning, my cheeks stretched so much they hurt. "Hey. It's so good to finally hear your voice."

"What's going on?" he asks.

"I'm just working," I say, not wanting to admit that I was in fact napping in the middle of the day. "Sorry I missed your calls earlier. I'm really glad you called back."

He lets out a laugh, the easy, carefree sound making me smile and easing some of my nerves. "No problem. I'm really excited to be talking to you. My heart was racing when I dialed your number. It still is."

I stall at those words, my heart skipping a beat at his admission. "It was? It is?"

"Yeah, beautiful, it is," he confirms.

Heat colors my cheeks and I reach for my electronic

cigarette, taking a quick puff. "I ... I don't know what to say to that."

He laughs again, this time a bit louder. "You don't have to say anything." There's a quick pause, and then, "Are you smoking? I didn't realize you were a smoker."

My eyes fall to the device in my hand. "I ... uh, I'm using an electronic cigarette. I've been trying to quit, but I still smoke the real thing, too. Is that a problem?"

"Yes," he says bluntly. "It's disgusting, not to mention bad for you. You should quit."

"I'm trying," I say again, nervously. "That's why I have the electronic cigarette."

"Good," he says. "So, tell me about your day."

I blink, hesitating. He wants to know about my day? I rack my brain, trying to think of something—anything—exciting to tell him, but I draw a blank.

"It was kind of boring," I tell him. "I don't really do much ... ever."

"It's not boring," he says. "Your life's exciting to me. You get to do whatever you want."

"Okay." I hesitate, trying to think of something interesting to tell him, but all that comes out is, "I went for lunch in Peggy's Cove, then hid in my office. I tried to work, and totally failed at it, and ended up falling asleep reading."

My response makes him laugh.

"See," I say, "I told you my life was boring."

"It's not boring, Victoria. It's perfect, just like you are."

I giggle—yes, giggle—at that. "Thank you."

"For what?"

"For saying I'm perfect," I say, feeling my face heating again. "That was ... sweet."

"No problem, beautiful."

The moment he calls me beautiful, my face lights up with a wide smile. "Your turn. Tell me all about your day. I want to know everything."

He rambles on, speaking so quickly that I only catch every few words, but I don't care. I love talking to him, or rather listening to him talk. I'm not sure what I expected, but this upbeat and overly excited man is not it.

Every few minutes a recording plays, stalling our conversation. A constant reminder that the call is being recorded and monitored, making me even more nervous. I think he knows it, too, because he's only asking me easy questions to answer, and he's not leaving any awkward silences on the line. I kind of love him for it.

He's talking about his family, and I can hear the love and devotion in his voice, when suddenly another recording, this one different from the others says, "You have one minute left."

My heart sinks all the way to my toes. I didn't realize these calls were timed and I'm nowhere near ready to get off the phone with him. Actually, I think I could talk to him all day long.

"Can I call you again?" he asks, his tone hesitant as though he's not sure if he should be asking.

"Sure," I respond right away. "Call me anytime you want."

"Okay, I'll call you right back."

I'm about to say okay when I hear a recording say, "The caller has hung up."

And then, my phone rings again.

****

Days pass by.

Days full of phone calls.

Days full of laughter.

Days full of letters.

Richard goes back to work, flying out to the head office in Toronto this time, and Joshua and I fall into a routine. And my life ... well, it begins to revolve around our fifteen-minute phone calls.

We talk about everything, from childhood memories, to work, to his case. We talk about food, friends, and family. We tell each other stories, divulging our most embarrassing moments, trying to one-up each other. We chat about movies, talk about first kisses and first dates. Joshua grills me on everything and anything, as though he won't rest until he knows every single one of my secrets.

And the days ... they just keep slipping by, melting into one another.

It's Monday, and at nine-thirty in the morning, I'm still in bed. It's raining outside, pouring actually, and I feel like hell. My throat hurts, my nose is running, and I've got a killer headache.

My phone rings as I'm lying there. I reach over to the nightstand, snatching it up and glancing at the screen to see Joshua's number. Sniffling, I answer it, waiting through the long recording and accepting the call.

"How's my beautiful angel doing?"

Sighing, I mutter, "Hey."

He's silent for a moment. "You okay, baby girl?"

"Yeah, why?"

"You sound like fucking shit."

His response makes a hoarse laugh rumble up my throat. "Thanks."

"That's your awkward laugh," he says. "What's wrong? What did I say to make you laugh like that?"

"How do you know my laughs?" I ask, trying not to smile, but one cracks my face. Geez, this man ...

"I just know," he says seriously. "Sometimes it feels like I've known you all my life."

"Really?"

"Yeah, baby, really." He pauses for a beat. "Now tell me what that laugh was about."

"I don't really know," I say. "You just make me nervous sometimes, I guess."

He lets out a deep sigh. My answer obviously doesn't reassure him either. Changing the subject, he says, "I've been thinking that you should come visit me ... if you want to. No pressure, but I'd really like to meet you."

The question stalls me and I hesitate. I'm not sure what to say. The idea excites and terrifies me. "I'm not sure that's such a good idea. Richard won't like it and ..."

"Do you want to come?" he asks, cutting me short.

I hesitate. "I do."

"Then it's settled," he says. "Pick a date."

5

Where Is My Phone?

"Please …" Becca whines from the large bowl chair behind me. She showed up about twenty minutes ago, letting herself into my house and planting herself in my office, dramatically demanding that we go out for a spa day. "You've been working too much lately," she whines. "The novel's almost done. You can afford to take the day off and come to the spa with me. Besides, I've already booked us in and the packages are non-refundable."

While I'm sure she's right, I have been working too much lately, I don't really want to go. I'm behind on my word count for the day and on top of that, I have two letters from Joshua sitting on my desk that I need to reply to. Spending the day at the spa really isn't high on my priority list.

I keep my attention on my emails, clicking my way through all the social media notifications. "I can't, Becca. I'm behind."

"You're always behind," she says with a long, drawn out huff. She comes up behind me, placing a hand on my shoulder. "Taking a few hours for yourself isn't going to ..." she stalls suddenly, her grip tightening on my shoulder. "Uh, Vic, why are you getting mail from a prison in the United States?"

I sigh, shrugging her hand off my shoulder, and then I turn around, leaning back in my chair and looking up at her. She's frowning, her nose wrinkled up as she stares at the letter sitting on top of the heaping stack of paperwork.

She doesn't look happy. Not even a little.

"Ummm ... research?" I say, though it comes out as a question rather than the sure statement it was meant to be.

Becca narrows her eyes, crossing her arms over her chest. "Want to try that one again?"

No. Not really. I'd really prefer not talking about it at all, but the hard glint in Becca's chocolatey brown eyes tells me that's not an option.

So much for keeping Joshua a secret.

"Well, it started as research ... kind of," I say, running a nervous hand through my hair. I haven't told anyone about Joshua, well, no one but Richard, and I have no idea what she'll think. "I was researching kidnapping cases for a book, and I stumbled on this prisoner pen-pal website, and ..."

"You have a prisoner pen-pal?" she half whispers, half shouts.

"Um ... yeah."

"Holy shit." Becca grins excitedly, surprising me because she isn't exactly the nonjudgmental type. "Turn off the computer," she says. "We're going to the spa. *Now.*"

I let out a sharp, nervous laugh. *Shit.* That's her *I'm not leaving you alone until you tell me everything* voice. I glance back at my computer screen. I know I should just tell her no, but Richard's home again, and the last thing I want to do is have this conversation while he's right across the hall working on that stupid boat-in-a-bottle.

"Fine, okay," I say, eventually. "I can't wait."

Forty-five minutes later, I'm sitting in a massaging chair with my feet submerged in warm water. Becca's beside me, her long blonde hair tied up in a messy bun. She has her phone in her hand, her nose scrunched up as she studies Joshua's pen-pal profile.

"Damn, girl," she mutters, her big brown eyes peeking up at me. "That man is hot. Does Richard know about him?"

I cut her a sideways look. "Of course he knows. Why would I hide that from him?"

"Because he's your husband, and this ..." she waves a hand at me dramatically, "is not really something you tell your husband about." Her eyes fall back onto Joshua's picture, a soft smile touching her lips. "How did he take it?"

I shrug. "He was fine with it at the beginning, you know, before I actually sent the letter. Now ... well, he doesn't like it. He spends a lot of time trying to convince me Joshua is scum. I think he's feeling threatened, maybe."

"Is Joshua scum?"

I don't respond immediately, considering my words carefully. "No, I don't think so. He's ... sweet, Becca. He listens to me, really listens. And," I pause, biting my bottom lip, "he calls me 'beautiful'. Every single day. And he likes my curves. Loves them, actually."

Becca's eyes widen. "Oh no."

I laugh awkwardly, confused. "What?"

"I know that look," she says.

My brows furrow. "What look?"

"That one," she says, pointing an accusing finger at me. "You like him."

"Of course I like him," I say, feeling a blush staining my cheeks. "We've been writing and talking for months now."

Becca curves one of her perfectly shaped brows. "No, you like him like him. Damn, Vic. What have you gotten yourself into here?"

My pedicurist taps my right leg, and I lift it, putting it on the footrest, trying not to squirm as she begins taking off the old polish. It sucks having ticklish feet.

"I don't really know," I say truthfully. "But I can tell you one thing, I haven't been this happy in years."

"So, what are you going to do?" she asks, cutting me

a look. "And your answer better involve finally leaving Dick."

I roll my eyes at her. Becca may tolerate Richard for my sake, but she's never liked him and she's never hidden it.

"I don't know," I tell her. "He knows I'm done, that I want out, but I'm just ... I'm just ..."

"Scared," Becca supplies. "You're scared."

"Yeah." And I really, truly am.

The spa day lasts way too long. Between Becca's nonstop talking and my brain racing with story ideas, I'm not entirely sure I'm going to make it through all the pampering. I need my nails to dry and a pen and a pad. No. Scratch that. What I need right now is for my phone to ring.

I haven't heard from Joshua all day and it's ... odd. Really odd.

Digging around in my purse, I search for my phone, wondering if maybe I just didn't hear it ring. I rifle, searching and searching, pulling items out, pushing them around. Where the hell is my phone?

****

When I finally get home, it's nearly six o'clock at night. I find my phone on my desk so I grab it, looking to see if I missed any calls and what I see on the screen makes my stomach sink. Twenty-six missed calls, all from Joshua.

I sit down at my desk, setting the phone right beside

me, and I open up my emails. I try to focus—I really, really try—but it's pointless. Between the soft classical music coming from Richard's hobby room and my silent phone taunting me, I get nothing done. Instead, I spend a whole lot of time glaring at my phone, willing it to ring.

It sucks that I can't call him.

No. Scratch that.

Sucks is not a strong enough word for the way it feels.

It's pure hell.

An hour slips by. I respond to three emails. Another thirty minutes, two more emails cleaned up from my inbox. I look at my phone again and check to make sure the ringer is on. Twenty more minutes slip by. I update my expense tracking spreadsheet.

And the evening drags on, falling into night.

I'm tired, exhausted actually. The yawns keep slipping out no matter how hard I try to swallow them down. I'm just about to give up for the night when the phone finally rings.

Grabbing it, my heart beats wildly as I spot Joshua's number on the screen. Quickly, I answer it and accept the call.

"You okay?"

No hello. No beautiful. And his voice is rough—harsher than normal. I'm stunned. My lips twitch and I fight hard not to frown.

"Yes," I respond, my voice guarded as my entire body coils tightly. "I'm okay."

"Where've you been?"

I swallow hard. He doesn't sound happy. Actually, I've never heard his voice this ... cold before. I feel it like a chill spreading down my spine.

My stomach knots. "I was out."

"Where the fuck have you been?" he demands, his tone dropping, impatient and biting.

I laugh sharply, my body heating at his words. What the hell has gotten into him? Sure, I missed some calls, but this ... this attitude is ridiculous.

"I was out," I repeat, nervous anger leaking out of my voice.

"I called you twenty-six times," he says. "You got a fucking cell phone. Why the fuck didn't you answer it?"

"I forgot my phone at home."

He exhales loudly, frustrated. "Where the fuck have you been, Victoria? I'm not going to ask you again."

"I went out," I say, exasperated. "What do you want? A goddamn play by play?"

He exhales again, just as loudly as the last one, but this time I'm pretty sure it's a forced calming breath. "Yes, I do. And watch your tone with me."

It's my turn to let out a frustrated breath. "I went to the spa, got my nails done, had a massage and a facial. Then I went to the bookstore, got coffee, walked around the mall a little, went for dinner. I was just out doing stuff."

"Did you have a good time?"

"Um, yeah ..." my voice drops low. "I guess."

"Good," he says, his tone still as hard as concrete. "Glad you're okay and you had a good time." He pauses, letting out another loud exhale. "I'm done talking to you right now."

"Joshua ..."

"No," he says, cutting me short. "I'm done."

"Wait," I say, hating the desperation I hear in my voice. "What do you mean you're done?"

But he doesn't respond. Instead, I hear the recording say, "The caller has hung up."

Pulling my phone away from my ear, I stare at it for a beat. I feel the sting of tears—damn tears—in my eyes, and my chest feels so unbelievably tight that it's hard to breathe.

Oh my God. I don't understand what just happened.

I sit in my chair, blinking fast and sniffling, staring at my phone. I don't know how long I sit there, my eyes glued to the screen, hoping it'll ring again. It's probably been only five minutes, but it feels like hours.

Taking a deep breath, I set my phone aside and head into the bathroom washing my tears away. I take my time, slathering on some moisturizer and brushing my teeth, and after a few minutes, I'm starting to feel normal again. A little less shaky.

When I come out, Richard is standing there leaning against the wall, hands stuffed in his blue jeans. He's smirking, his shoulders are shaking with silent laughter, and looking at him, at the knowing look in his eyes, I know he was eavesdropping.

My temper flares white-hot.

"What's wrong?" he asks, his smirk stretching, turning into a full-blown smile. "You get into a fight with your little convict?"

I glare at him, long and hard. "Don't call him that," I say sharply, enunciating every single syllable. "He has a name."

Richard only laughs, and I spin around, walking back into my office, slamming the door behind me.

God, I hope he doesn't stay long.

6

Best Sex Ever

It's been a long day, mostly because I barely slept last night. My stupid brain kept replaying the conversation with Joshua over and over, trying to make sense out of it, but yeah, I couldn't. Still can't. We're friends. *Just friends.* And friends don't freak out when someone doesn't answer the phone.

When I gave up on sleeping, I spent a few hours seriously considering shutting down the phone line, and cancelling my prepaid calling account. The problem with that, though, is that every time I think about not hearing his voice again, my heart feels like it's cracking.

Then, I spent a few more hours trying to figure out what I did that was so horrible that he'd yell at me the way he had, wondering how I can fix it, and if he'll even give me the chance to try.

Ugh. Who am I kidding? We're not just friends. We're ... well, I don't know what we are, but *just friends* isn't it.

The cold hard truth? I'm ... attached and I don't want it to be over, but the question remains: what is *it*?

It's a little after two o'clock in the afternoon and I'm hiding in my office since Richard's still home. I can hear him cursing from across the hall. The boat project must not be going well today. He hasn't done his laundry or picked up his dry cleaning yet, so I assume he's staying overnight, but he won't tell me either way.

I should be working, but I can't concentrate. I've been checking my phone constantly since I woke up this morning, making sure it's on, checking if the ringer is turned up.

I'm agonizing, I know.

I don't know what to do about the argument.

I don't know what to do with myself.

I glare down at my phone again, because it hasn't rung all day, not that I expect it to. After the way Joshua ended things last night, I won't be surprised if I never hear from him again.

A shrill ring echoes through the room. My heart stops, and then races. I snatch up my phone, my heart stalling for a second before I glance at the caller display.

Please be him. Please be him. Please be him.

It's him. Holy shit! It's him. He's calling.

My heart thunders in my chest, beating like a jackhammer as I answer it, impatiently waiting for the recording to end, for my chance to accept the call.

"How's my beautiful angel doing?" Joshua says as soon as the line clicks through. He sounds upbeat today, happy even.

Not what I expected. Not at all.

I hesitate. "I'm fine. How are you?"

I'm a mess really, but I'm not about to admit it.

"I don't believe you," he says. "You're a shitty liar, baby girl. You're still mad about yesterday, aren't you?"

Despite myself, I smile at that. I can't believe how well this man knows me.

"You yelled at me," I say quietly. "Then you hung up on me and I thought I wasn't going to hear from you again. So, yeah, Joshua, I'm a little mad."

"You didn't answer your phone," he says simply. "You need to learn."

I snort out a laugh. "Are you kidding me right now? I'm not always going to be around to answer the phone for you."

"You should be," he says, a tinge of irritation seeping into his voice. "I waited in line for hours yesterday. People watched me wait in line and call you over and over, and you didn't pick up your fucking phone. It's fucking embarrassing. You wasted my time. You made me look like an idiot."

I blink. I don't even know what to say to that.

Embarrassed. He yelled at me because he was embarrassed. Really?

"You always pick up every time I call," he continues, "and when you didn't, I got extremely worried about you. I didn't know if something happened to you or if you and Richard got into a fight. I've lost a lot of people while I've been locked up and I was afraid I'd lost you, too. I caught feelings for you, baby girl, and I thought something happened to you and there was nothing I could do about it. I was fucking worried, and when you finally picked up, you were being a bitch about it. I've showed you the sweet loving side to me because I felt like you deserved it. It's a side that not too many people get to see, but I'm not going to let some bitch speak to me like you did yesterday."

"Really, you're calling me a bitch now?"

"You were being a bitch yesterday."

"I'm sorry," I mutter. And I am. The truth is, I've been sorry since I realized I forgot my phone.

Joshua laughs, all seriousness gone from his tone. "Say it again, this time try to make it believable."

"I'm not sure I can do that yet," I say teasingly, laughter in my voice. "Give me an hour or two, okay?"

My response makes him laugh again, this time a full, loud laugh. It's an amazing sound, packed full of raw energy and when he speaks again, his voice is deeper than normal. "Is your pussy wet, baby?"

I blink and let out an awkward laugh, surprised by the question. Some of our calls and letters have touched on sexual stuff, but he's never been this blunt before. What is he doing here?

"No," I say after a moment, though my voice doesn't come out nearly as confident as I would have liked. The truth is, as soon as he asked, I could feel the dampness gather between my legs.

He hums. "Again with the lying. I hope this doesn't become a habit." He pauses for a beat, and when I say nothing, he continues. "Stick your hand in your panties and tell me."

"No," I repeat, this time a little firmer. "Joshua, I can't do this with you." And I can't. Even if Richard wasn't home, playing with that stupid boat right across the hallway from my office, engaging in phone sex just isn't right.

I'm still married.

I still live with my husband—kind of.

It's just ... not right, even if Richard knows it's over between us.

Joshua chuckles. "Yes you can. I know you want to be my little slut. Be a good girl and reach into those panties. I want you to tell me how wet your pussy is."

I swallow hard, feeling heat coil through my body. Shit, I want to. I really, really want to, but again I say, "I can't. We can't. Richard's home and ..."

He doesn't listen to me. Actually, he right out ignores me, cutting me off. "You know what I'm picturing? I'm picturing you in nothing but a garter belt and thigh high sheer stockings. You've got on a pair of stiletto heels, and you're in the kitchen cooking me dinner."

I laugh awkwardly. "No one cooks dinner in a garter belt, stockings, and heels."

Again he ignores me. "I walk up behind you, slapping your ass once nice and hard, and then I lean down and start kissing your neck."

"Please stop," I whisper, though I don't mean it, and he hears it. He knows.

"You don't really want me to stop, do you, baby girl?"

I don't respond, but I don't have to. This man who has only known me through letters and a handful of phone calls knows me better than anyone else. He knows me better than anyone ever has.

I'm not sure how I feel about that.

"I grab you by the hips, spinning you around, and back you up against the wall. My hands slide around, cupping that perfect ass of yours, squeezing hard as I lift you up, telling you to wrap those thick thighs around my waist."

My heartbeat picks up, thrumming away in my chest, and I make a sound somewhere between a moan and a whimper.

If he hears it, he doesn't let on. "I dip my head, taking one of your hard nipples into my mouth, biting down, then sucking the sting away, before moving on to your other perfect breast. After I'm done sucking on your nipples, I walk you over to the kitchen table, and in one solid motion I knock everything off, and set you down.

I kiss my way down your body until I'm on my knees, placing your legs on my shoulders. Then, I start kissing the inside of one of your thighs until I reach your pussy, making sure it's nice and wet. I stick my tongue inside your cunt, tasting your juices and trailing my fingers up your legs to your inner thighs, gliding a finger into your tight pussy while my tongue starts doing circles on your clit."

My stomach is in knots, and my breath is short. Jesus, what is this man doing to me? I've never been so turned on before. My hands are shaking and my voice whispers softly as I say, "You make me so wet."

And it's true. I don't have to reach into my panties to feel the wetness—I'm so saturated I can feel it soaking them.

It's unreal.

It's amazing.

I've always had trouble getting wet with Richard. It doesn't matter how much foreplay we have, we still need lube. But with Joshua, all he has to do is say a few words and my pussy is soaking.

"Good," he says. "Touch yourself for me, baby. Rub your clit a little."

"Okay," I whimper, my voice cracking on the word. God, I feel like a gawky teenager, all shaky and blushing. But ... my pussy has never, and I mean never, been this soaked.

I undo my jeans, hesitantly reaching down and running

a finger along my clit. It's throbbing, my wet channel clenching, begging to be filled.

"I start working my tongue faster, flicking your clit," he says. "Every time I pull my fingers in and out of your pussy, you moan a little louder and your legs start shaking on my shoulders. I know you're liking what I'm doing. Your nails are digging into my head. I know you're ready to come, so I keep moving faster, thrusting my fingers in and out, until your pussy starts to clench and you come around my digits."

Gasping at the image, I rub my clit and pump my fingers inside me. My body shudders, and my heart races. I want more, need more. More of him.

"Once you finish coming, I pull my fingers out of your pussy, standing up and sticking them into your mouth, telling you to lick them clean. Then, I undo my jeans, taking my hard cock out. It's dripping with pre-come and I press it deep inside you. Baby, I love how wet and tight your pussy is. As I'm working my hips back and forth, I dip my head sucking on one of your hard nipples, and then the other."

Pleasure explodes inside of me, unlike anything I've ever felt before. I close my eyes, swallowing down the moan that's creeping up my throat. I'm close, so, so close ...

"I grab your throat, and my lips meet yours, my tongue darts into your mouth as my other hand grips your ass. I start fucking you harder, slamming my cock in and out of your tight cunt. Your hand goes down to your clit and you start rubbing it. Our warm bodies are pressed so tight, our hearts racing in our chests, and I feel like I'm going to come, but I want you to come again, so I lean down, whispering in your ear, "Come for me, my little slut."'

And I do. My orgasm grabs me, and I let out a soft moan, arching my back as my wet walls convulse. "I'm coming," I say, though my voice is barely a whisper.

Joshua pauses, giving me a moment to catch my breath. I relax back in my seat, panting as the sensation subsides, my body feeling like Jell-O.

We're both quiet for a moment, my breathing, the only sound filling the line between us. When he speaks again, his voice is soft and sweet. "Did you come good, baby girl?"

"Yes," I whisper, and then I say, "Yes, thank you."

"Anytime, baby."

And then, the one-minute warning plays on the line.

"I'm going to go jerk off," he says. "I'll call you later."

"Okay," I say, and then he hangs up.

I set down the phone, slowly doing up my pants, before curling up into my chair, resting my head on the plush pillow. I never thought that the steamiest sex I'd ever have would be on my phone.

Shit. What did I just do?

I'm a horrible, horrible person.

7

New Hobbies and Garden Shears

———————

"My legs hurt."

Joshua laughs. "I'm sorry, baby. You still driving?"

"Yes," I mutter, readjusting in my seat. Note to self, indoor spin class equals muscle agony. "It's like my legs are on fire, and I hurt *everywhere*. I don't know why I thought this was a good idea."

Okay, that's not entirely true. I know exactly why I thought trying out a spin class was a good idea. Not only has my weight loss slowed down over the last couple of weeks and spinning is supposed to be a great cardio workout, but I figured that it might be easier than running since there's a seat.

I was totally wrong.

"You did it because you needed to change up your

workout," he says, his tone hinting at his amusement. "Don't be a pussy about it. When you get home, put some BENGAY on your legs. They'll feel better."

"Right," I say, squirming a little more as I flick on my signal, changing lanes. Then, feeling a little uncomfortable complaining to him about how out of shape I am and wanting to talk about something, anything but my burning muscles, I say, "I have a question for you."

"Shoot."

"If you found a spider in your house," I say, pulling up to a stop light, "would you kill it or put it outside?"

He laughs. "Well, I've been bitten by two poisonous spiders, so I'd kill it. Where did that come from?"

The light changes to green, and I give the car some gas. "I'm not really sure. It just came to me."

He laughs again. "Aww, changing the subject. Was I making you uncomfortable, beautiful?"

"Maybe a little bit," I mumble, feeling my face flush. I don't know what it is about him calling me beautiful that makes me squirm, but damn, I like it. I like it a lot. "So what are your plans for the day?"

"I've got REC at eleven, twelve your time," he says, still chuckling under his breath. "If a movie's on later, I'll probably watch that, but other than that, my day's wide open. You?"

"Not really sure yet." I hesitate, running through my schedule in my mind. "I'll probably work for a bit, but Richard was still home when I left, so ..."

"Really? Doesn't he have to work?"

"I don't know. I asked, but all he'd say was that he was going back to work when he felt like it."

Joshua lets out an aggravated huff. "I don't know how you put up with his shit. It drives me crazy knowing that you're stuck there with him, dealing with him, and there's nothing I can do about it. You really need to start thinking about getting out, beautiful. Make a plan."

"Yeah, I guess I do," I agree, because he's right. I do need to make a plan, an exit strategy of sorts.

Joshua keeps talking, rambling on about the weather and his workout. He tells me what's on the menu for the day, grumbling about how much he hates fish and mayo, and I fill him in on all the errands I have to run, and the housekeeping I've been slacking on. The conversation flows easily, just falling from the tongue naturally, and it strikes me, when was the last time I've felt so comfortable with someone that we could fill a conversation with mindless chatter without getting bored? I can hardly remember.

Maybe never.

When I pull into the driveway, the garage is wide open. Richard is there, standing in front of the house, eyeing my rosebushes with what looks like a pair of garden shears in hand.

I freeze, my hand resting on the gear shift as my eyes take in the mess. I'm guessing he's been out here for a while because the beautiful bushes have been ... trimmed, half the blossoms now covering the lawn.

My rosebushes.

The rosebushes I planted when I moved in with him.

Really?

Stomach sinking, I let go of the gear shift, turning off the car, eyeing Richard cautiously. "Joshua, I think I have to go. Richard's, uh ... outside, and it looks like he's gardening."

"Really?" Joshua sounds confused. "He's gardening?"

"Well ..." I hesitate. "He's doing something with the garden."

"Is there a problem?" Joshua asks, his tone changing, hardening.

"Not sure yet," I tell him. "I'm sure it's nothing. He's probably just in a mood. I'll talk to you later, okay?"

"No," he says. "I want to stay on the phone with you. Make sure everything's okay."

"I, uh ..." His tone is chilling, cold and angry. I have no idea how to make him feel okay again, what to say to bring back the playful, talkative man from moments ago. *Shit.* I shouldn't have said anything. "It's fine. I'll be fine."

"Victoria ..."

"It's fine," I repeat, cutting him short. "I can handle him. Besides, you can't do ..." I stall mid-sentence, biting off the words, hoping like hell I didn't offend him.

Way to make him feel better, Vic.

Ugh, I'm such an insensitive bitch.

"Right," he says, his voice losing all emotion, turning blank. "You're right, there's nothing I can do. Just don't let him push you around, okay? Stand up for yourself."

"Okay."

He mumbles a goodbye, and then the line clicks and the familiar recording plays in my ear indicating that he hung up. Groaning, I shove my phone into my purse, and run my hands over my face, frustrated. *Shit.* Why is Richard even still here?

I reach into my purse, digging around for the pack of cigarettes and lighter, knowing that the electronic one isn't going to cut it right now, before I get out of the car and start toward him, lighting one up. He's watching me, his expression blank as he opens up the shears and takes another random snip out of my flowers.

My footsteps falter as the yellow blossoms fall to the ground, and I take a drag from my cigarette. Richard's eyes are puffy and red, his nose slightly swollen. His allergies are kicking his ass. From where I'm standing, I can see that three of the once beautiful bushes have been torn right out at the roots, which explains the redness spreading up his arms.

Shit. Shit. Shit.

What the hell is he doing?

"Are you okay?" I ask, stepping onto the lawn, approaching him cautiously.

"I'm great," he says, and takes another snip out of the

flowers. He tips his head toward the destroyed bushes. "What do you think?"

I blink, taking another puff. *What do I think?*

"I don't know," I say, shaking my head, because I truly don't know what to think. "Why are you doing this?"

Richard shrugs. "I figured I needed a new hobby. Becoming a gardener sounds ... appealing."

Grimacing, I scan him over as an uneasy chill spreads up my spine. "What's wrong with you?"

"Absolutely nothing," he says. He's silent for a moment, regarding me, looking none too impressed that I'm still standing here. "Don't you have work to do?"

I hesitate, staring at him for a moment, not sure what to do. He looks like he needs his medication, but he's irritated about something and I most definitely do not want to deal with that.

Sighing, I eventually nod and put out my cigarette. "Yeah, I do. Do you want me to grab your allergy meds before I get started though?"

"Nah," he says, smirking at me. "I'm good."

I stall for another second, eyeing him carefully, before heading straight for the door. I slip into the house and shut it behind me, so he doesn't decide to follow me. Running a hand through my hair, I head up the stairs, my footsteps faltering when I reach my office. The typically closed door is wide open. I pause a few feet away, scanning the room, noting the shredded paper scattered all over the floor and the always locked filing cabinet with the drawers hanging open.

My eyes glue to it and a legitimate feeling of surprise passes over me, although it's wiped away by fury just as quickly. Shaking my head for a moment, I stare at the broken lock, before my feet start to move.

Rushing into my office, I pause at the first shreds of paper, recognizing the colorful scraps immediately.

Joshua's letters.

That asshole!

He tore up Joshua's letters.

Fury induced tears burn my eyes as I move over to my filing cabinet. It's a mess. Files dumped, papers scattered. I dig through the mess, searching for my photo album, hoping like hell that the bastard didn't destroy that too.

After a moment of searching, I find it laying open to Joshua's picture at the bottom of the pile. My gaze locks on it, my throat closing as I see the state of the photo and Richard's poor captioning job. Joshua is now sporting devil horns and there's a caption bubble that reads: I've killed and I'm okay with it.

My heart thundering in my ears, I pivot in place, not bothering to drop my purse before jogging back down the stairs. Anger overwhelms me, heating my skin, blurring my vision. It spreads through me like a wild fire, burning me up.

"You broke into my filing cabinet." The words fly from

my mouth as I rip open the front door, stepping out onto the covered porch. "Who the fuck do you think you are?"

"Of course I did," he says, smirking at me from his spot by the garden. "I know everything. Every-*fucking*-thing."

I let out a sharp laugh. "You don't know anything."

"I searched your computer, too," he says casually. "I read all of those letters you wrote him. You're a goddamn fool, Vic, falling for all his bullshit."

I roll my eyes, throwing my hands up in the air. "I'm not *falling* for anything."

"You love him," he says, matter-of-factly. "You fell in love with a convict."

His statement freezes my rage. Did I? I don't know. I like Joshua. No. Scratch that. It's more than *like*. I care about him—a lot. But love?

I don't know.

At the moment, I don't even know what to do or what to say or even what to think.

I laugh because I can't dispute his claims and there's really no point in lying about it—I like Joshua. I care about him a lot, so much so that I'm terrified to admit it. And from the way Richard's eyes are searching me, and that goddamn smirk on his lips, I'm pretty sure he can see it. He knows how I feel.

"You're going to make yourself sick out here," I mutter after a moment, spotting the beginning of what looks like hives spreading up his arms. "Take your pills and go to bed. We can talk about this later."

"There's nothing to talk about," he hisses. "It's either me or him, but fair warning, if you decide to leave me for some fucking killer, I'll take you for everything you have. I'll take your business, this house, every goddamn cent in your bank account. I'll take everything and make sure you don't get even a goddamn penny of my money."

I laugh harshly, feeling the red-hot rage flare once more. "Don't you dare threaten me."

"It's not a threat," he says, dropping the gardening shears to the ground. "It's a promise. You choose to keep talking to that biker and I'll take everything from you."

"The choice isn't between you and him." Heat rushes through my body as my hands curl into white-knuckled fists, although when I speak again, my voice comes out scary calm. "It's between me and you, and you know what, Richard, for the first time since I met you, I'm choosing me."

He narrows his eyes, taking a long stride toward me. "What the fuck is that supposed to mean?"

I don't respond right away, glaring at him, my thoughts racing as I attempt to pick my words carefully. I open my mouth, close it, open it once more, and then my phone rings.

Pulling it out of my purse, I glance at the caller display, not surprised to see Joshua's number flashing there. I know I shouldn't answer it. I know it will only piss Richard off further, but I do it anyway.

Maybe it's because I don't care if it pisses him off.

Or maybe it's because I want it to.

I'm not really sure.

"Hey, beautiful," Joshua says as soon as the call connects, his voice instantly soothing my nerves. "Is everything okay?"

"Hey, I'm not really sure yet, but it will be."

He's quiet for a moment. "What's going on?"

"Nothing," I say, trying my damnedest to keep my voice light and cheery. I'm pretty sure I fail. "Everything's fine. I'm just in the middle of something with Richard. I'll talk to you later, okay?"

A moment of silence, and then, "Fine. I'm going to call back in twenty minutes," he says, although he doesn't sound happy about letting me go. "Please, even if you're not done, answer the phone and tell me you're okay."

A genuine smile splits my lips. This man …

"Okay," I say softly. "I will."

"Talk to you soon."

"Bye."

Hanging up and dropping the phone back into my purse, I turn my attention back to my *so-called* husband, glaring at him. I take a deep breath, and then I answer his question. "What it means is that it's about time I do something that makes me happy, Richard, and stop worrying about what you think."

Red tints his already swollen face, and he balls his hands into white-knuckled fists. "You didn't seem to give a fuck about what I thought when you quit your job and started writing fulltime."

I snort out a laugh. "I did that for you. You're the one who was embarrassed that I was a waitress, not me. I loved that job. And don't act like that wasn't the best career decision for me."

Richard sneezes so loud it makes me jump. He wipes his nose with the back of his hand. "It wasn't. It gave you too much time on your hands, and look at what you did with that time."

Shaking my head, I sigh. God, I almost feel sorry for him. *Almost.* "For a few years now, I've been living my life trying to make you happy, trying to make you proud of me. I worked like a dog fulltime, and started publishing books to make more money because that's what was important to you. Then, I quit a job I loved because it embarrassed you. I gave up friends and I barely speak to my family because you don't like them. I moved to this ostentatious, oversized house because you needed to have everything better than everyone else. I do everything you want, killing myself to try to make you happy, and you do nothing but ignore me and degrade me. It doesn't matter what I do, it's still not good enough. Nothing's ever good enough for you, and I'm done trying."

"You're done trying," he says coolly, closing the distance between us, stalling a mere few feet from me. "Sorry you think I'm such a shitty husband."

And then he walks past me and into the house, and

moments later, I hear what I hope is the bedroom door slamming shut.

My stomach clenches. I'm not sure if it's from the door slamming or the guilt that's twisting me up.

Did he just look hurt?

I hurt him?

I hurt Richard.

I...

I'm not sure how long I stand there before I head back inside, kicking off my shoes and strolling back upstairs, arms crossed over my chest. I go into my office, kicking the door shut behind me. It couldn't have been too long because Joshua hasn't called yet, but it feels like forever.

I glance at the mess before dropping my purse and curling up in my chair, staring blankly out the window, listening to Richard's muffled snoring coming from across the hallway, feeling more alone than I've ever felt before.

I don't know why I feel guilty.

I shouldn't, I know.

I've been honest with Richard from the start. He knew—he knows—how I feel. He knows I want out. He knows it's over.

God, I need to get out of here.

When my phone finally rings, I answer it immediately. Grabbing my keys, I head back downstairs, slipping on my shoes and walking out the door, locking it behind me as I wait for my chance to accept the call. As soon as the call connects, Joshua's voice surrounds me like a warm fleece blanket. "Hey, beautiful. You done yet?"

"Yeah, I'm done," I say. "He's passed out now."

"What's happening?

"He kind of broke into my filing cabinet and read, then tore up, all of your letters," I say, walking down the driveway, and onto the sidewalk. I feel restless ... uneasy. A walk is exactly what I need even if every step feels like torture. Damn that cycling class. "I think that's why he decided to destroy my rosebushes."

"I'm not surprised," he says. "So what did he have to say about the letters?"

Sighing, I reply, "Nothing really, but he's under the impression that I'm in love with you."

He's quiet for a moment. "Are you?"

My blood runs hot at his question. "What? I, uh ..." I don't know what to say. "No. I'm not in love with you. I barely even know you."

"Baby girl, you know me better than anyone ever has, but if you don't want to admit your feelings yet, no problem. I can wait." He chuckles softly, before continuing, "So he's feeling threatened by me."

Yeah, and he's also threatening to take everything from me.

I don't tell him that, though, instead saying, "It doesn't make sense. He never gave a shit before. Not about anything I did."

"Yeah, but now you've got another man in your life," he

says lightly, and then his tone turns serious. "I'm sorry he ruined all the letters, baby."

"Yeah," I grumble, annoyed and more than a little sad that I didn't take better care of them. "Me, too."

8

I'm Not Jealous

"Have you picked a date to come see me yet?"

Taking in the harsh voice that greets me when I accept the call, I turn my desk chair around, placing my back to the computer screen, and I give Joshua my full attention. He sounds on edge today, a little amped up and a little annoyed. I'm not sure what to make of it.

"Not yet," I say hesitantly. "I've been thinking maybe November would be good, but I'm still trying to rearrange my schedule. Um, are you okay?"

The line is stone cold silent for a moment before his voice carries through. "I got a letter today."

Okay ...

"That's awesome," I say, trying to keep my voice light and cheery. It's a challenge. "I'm glad, honey."

Silence.

"Don't you want to know about it?"

I don't respond immediately, my gaze scanning the books on my shelves, the question lingering on the silent line between us. After a moment, I sigh. "No, not really."

"Why?"

Why? I'm not even sure I can answer that. I've thought about Joshua's other pen-pals a lot these last few weeks, pretty much every single day since that first time we had phone sex, and I can only come up with one logical conclusion: I want to pretend there aren't any others. "Because it's really none of my business."

"Why's that?" he asks.

"Because it just isn't," I say. "Besides, I don't particularly want to hear about the other women in your life."

He hums. "I thought I could talk to you about anything. Isn't that what you told me?"

I sigh again, this time long and loud as I recall that particular conversation. After a long pause, I say tentatively, "You can."

And I mean it for the most part. I want to know everything there is to know about him, see every side of him, dig deep down and understand everything that makes him who he is. But those letters ... I don't think I can handle knowing what's in those letters.

"Obviously not," he says.

The disappointment I hear in his voice makes my chest constrict. "Is this letter really that important?"

"Yes."

"Fine." My voice sounds snappy even to my own ears, but I can't help it, can't seem to smooth it out. I take a breath and then another. It does nothing to soothe the anxiety blooming in my chest. "Okay, fine. If it's that important, tell me about it."

"Someone's getting a little bitchy," he says almost playfully—almost. "Is your period starting soon?"

His comment startles a laugh from me. Did he really just say that? "You can be such an ass sometimes; you know that?"

"I know." He laughs, and then stalls for a beat. "Are you jealous of the letters I get, baby?"

I roll my eyes. So, that's his game here. He's trying to make me jealous. Even so, it stuns me how easily he reads me, even over the phone. He sounds so edgy, but still so damn confident. I wish I had his confidence, wish I could speak my mind the same way he does, holding nothing back. "I'm not jealous."

"So that's how it's going to be? You're going to lie to me now?" He hums his disapproval. "Come on, beautiful. If you've got something to say, now is the time."

I hesitate, not sure what to tell him. It's been nearly a week since Richard went back to work. Nearly a week since he violated my privacy and destroyed my office. It's been nearly a week since I told Joshua I don't love him.

Since I told Joshua I don't love him ...

I blink, swallowing down a startled laugh, the pieces falling into place. Jesus, is he feeling insecure?

I take a breath.

And another.

And then another.

"Just tell me about the letter," I say, although I feel anxiety bubbling in my stomach as the words slip out of my mouth. "Who was it from?"

"Melissa."

That's it. That's all he says as though the name answers all the unspoken questions filling the air between us.

My brow furrows. "Which one is that again?"

"I dated her, remember?" he says. "The one that decided she couldn't wait for me to get out, and hooked up with someone else. They broke up and she started writing me again. She's the one I told about you."

Great. That's the one that's been trying to convince him to take her back. The last he told me, though, was that he had sent her a letter using me as an out, telling her he was in a committed relationship.

"Oh, right. The one you lied to about us."

My response makes him laugh, though it's not an amused sound. "She said she's happy that I found you, but she hopes it doesn't work out so she can be with me. She told me she loves me and wants to marry me. She even hinted that she'd like to get married before I get released."

I stop breathing at those words, and for a second my heart feels as though it stops right along with my lungs.

And then ... it races.

My skin flushes and my eyes begin to sting. I blink fast, banishing away the threatening tears as I suck in a breath.

This man ... this man *is* trying to make me jealous.

If I didn't think it before, I'm convinced now.

This is my punishment for letting my marriage fail. Finding what could very well be an epic love, and then watching it vanish before it has a chance to turn into what it could be. *What it's meant to be.*

"Why are you telling me this?" I whisper eventually.

"Because."

He says nothing more. Just *because* as though that's an answer in itself.

Maybe it is.

Or maybe he's just being an ass.

"Because why?" I ask, although I'm almost certain I don't want to hear the answer.

"Because you're my best friend," he says simply. "Who else am I supposed to tell?"

Anyone. "What else did she have to say?"

"That she'd be a good wife, cooking and cleaning and taking care of all my needs."

I'm sure she would.

"Maybe you should give her a shot, that is, if you think she'll actually stick it out this time around."

"Is that what you want me to do?" he asks curiously.

I laugh dryly, slipping out of my chair and standing up.

My legs are wobbly, my knees weak. Damn this stupid conversation.

Ugh, I need a smoke (or ten).

"It doesn't really matter what I want," I say, walking out of my office and down the stairs. "You do whatever it is you want to do."

"I *will* do whatever I want," he says. "Doesn't mean I don't want your opinion."

I head through the quiet house, letting silence fill the line as I grab my cigarettes off the counter, and then I open the patio door and step out into the backyard. Walking across the lawn, I stop at the pool, sitting down and letting my feet dangle in the cool water as I light one up, inhaling deeply. "I'm not sure what you want me to say here."

"Are you smoking?" he asks.

"Uh …" I glance down at my cigarette, watching the smoke curl from the lit end. "Yeah, I'm smoking."

"I hope you're using the e-cigarette."

"Nope," I mutter, taking another long drag, soothing my nerves. "I'm sitting at the pool with my feet in the water, smoking a real cigarette."

"Why?" he asks, a hint of annoyance in his voice. "I thought you were quitting that shit."

"I am," I say, taking another drag. "I just want a real one right now."

"Baby," he says, drawing out the word. "Don't get all stressy. We're just tal …"

His voice is cut off mid-word, the goddamn recording letting us know that we only have one minute left.

"There's a line-up for the phone," he says, once the recording ends. "I'll call you back as soon as I can get back on."

"You don't have to wait in line," I mumble. "We can just talk tomorrow or whatever."

"No," he responds instantly. "I'm not done talking to you. I'll call you back."

He hangs up then, and I let out a long sigh, setting my phone down on the travertine pool deck, and swishing my legs back and forth through the water. I don't know how long it takes for the phone to ring again. It could be seconds, minutes, even an hour. I'm not sure. I'm dazed, feeling lost, and so damn lonely it hurts.

It hurts a lot.

So much so my chest feels constricted.

Is this it? Could it really be over before it even starts? Do I even care if it is?

My expression falls. Yes, I care. I care far more than I should.

When the phone rings, I answer it right away, lighting up another cigarette as I wait out the recording for my chance to accept the call. As soon as the call clicks through, he says, "Tell me what you're thinking."

No *hey, beautiful*, no real greeting at all. I shouldn't be surprised, the last call was the same, but I am.

Shit. Two calls and I'm already missing his sweet greetings.

I sigh, rolling my cigarette between my fingers. "I'm thinking that you're trying to make me jealous. I'm thinking this is your way of digging, trying to find out if I'd give a shit if you start dating someone."

"Would you give a shit?" he asks.

The question stalls me and I hesitate, frowning. I take another drag of my cigarette. "Of course I would. I care about you a lot, Joshua. But I can't stand in your way. And it really bugs me that I don't have a right to say anything about it."

"You're right," he says. "You don't have a right to say anything about it."

He doesn't need to say anything else, although I hear the unspoken words as though he yelled them at me.

You're married.

You still live with your husband.

"I hate it," I say. "I fucking hate that I can't stop you from starting something up with her. But it doesn't change anything."

"Aww, how cute. My baby girl is jealous." He chuckles, but when he speaks again, his voice is serious. "You're going to leave him, right?"

"Yeah, I'm going to leave him," I say honestly. "It'll be months, maybe even a year before I get everything in order, but I'm going to leave."

"Promise?"

"Yes, I promise."

"Then it's settled," he says, and I can actually hear the satisfied grin cracking his face. "I'll tell her I'm not interested."

"Are you sure you can handle dealing with this?" I ask. "It's going to take time. It's going to be hard."

"You sure you can handle waiting four years for me to get out?" he counters.

"I think so."

"Then I think so, too." He pauses, and when he speaks again, his voice is playful. "Are you still at the pool?"

I hesitate, my forehead scrunching up at the question. "Um, yeah."

"Why don't you take that sexy fat ass of yours back inside and up to your bedroom, and grab your vibrator."

His words make me freeze. "Did you just call my ass fat?"

"Baby," he says, drawing out the word. "That's just how I talk and you know I fucking love that you've got a big ass and hips. It's sexy. You're fucking sexy. Now, hurry up. I'm horny."

"No," I say, shaking my head. And I'm not sexy. Not even a little. "Not now. I just don't feel like it."

He laughs lightly. "Yes."

"I'm really not in the mood, Joshua," I protest. "Can't we just talk for a bit?"

"If you're going to be my girl," he says, "then you need to understand that when it comes to sex the answer's always yes. Go get your toy, beautiful. You'll feel better once you come. Promise."

The words make me stall, my heart thumping so hard that it makes me dizzy. *His girl*. It's the first time he's ever referred to me as anything close to that. A silence falls over the line as he waits for me to respond, and I glance toward the house, pulling my legs out of the pool and standing up. "Okay."

"Good, now hurry up before the call cuts off again."

He doesn't say anything else as I jog inside and up the stairs, and doesn't make a sound as I open the drawer, retrieving my vibrator. Quickly I undress, dropping my clothes onto the floor as I climb up into bed. He must hear the rustling of the bed sheets, because he asks, "You ready, sweetness?"

"Um ... yeah, I'm ready."

"Good," he says, sounding pleased. "I want you to turn that vibrator on and rest it on your clit. Get your pussy nice and wet for me, baby."

That does it.

I'm officially in the mood.

I shiver, turning on the vibrator. My lips part, and I let out a small, little gasp, as I rub it against my clit, whispering, "Okay."

"Good girl," he says. "Now tell me what you're picturing."

"I, uh ... I..." I'm nervous, stammering, stumbling over my words. Ugh, if we keep doing this, I'm going to have to call one of those phone sex lines for some pointers. "I ... I don't know."

"I'm picturing you, hands gripping the bed, ass sticking out. Your pussy is already nice and wet, and I drop down behind you. I start kissing your ass as my hands glide down your thighs. My fingers reach your pussy and I slide a finger inside your tight channel, making my cock nice and hard."

I moan softly, feeling the wetness gather between my legs. I really don't know what it is about this man, but he turns me on.

Really turns me on.

It's electric.

"I pull my fingers out of your pussy," he says, "sticking them into my mouth, and telling you how good you taste, before I stand up and place my cock at your entrance. With one thrust, I slam my dick deep inside you, my balls smacking against your clit, and you moan nice and loud."

My heart hammers as I slide my vibrator inside me, letting out a shuddering breath. My eyes flutter closed. I can almost feel his hands on me, his body surrounding me.

I want more.

Need more.

"I reach up, wrapping your hair around my fist and I pull nice and hard, making your back arch and your ass press against me. As I pull my cock out, and slam it back in, your ass starts to shake and your hands grip the sheets. Baby, your pussy is so wet I can feel your juices dripping down my balls."

A strange thrill rushes through me as his voice fills the line. I'm caught in a whirlwind. There's really no other way to explain what I'm feeling. I'm moaning, writhing on the bed, barely even remembering that it's my hands touching my skin and not his.

It's unreal.

It's amazing.

"You want more, baby girl?" he asks.

"Yes!" I nearly scream the word at him. "Yes, please ... Please don't stop. I'm close. So close."

He chuckles softly, a sexy, throaty sound. "I smack your ass nice and hard as I pull my cock out and slam it back in. I reach around and start rubbing your clit, pinching it between my fingers. As your pussy muscles spasm around my cock, I start fucking you harder, flicking your clit with my finger. Your legs start to shake, my dick starts to twitch deep inside you, and you look back at me, telling me to fill your pussy with my come. It turns me on so fucking much that my balls begin to lift. Your pussy starts to tighten around my cock, and then you moan, legs shaking as you come, making my cock harden and shoot warm come deep inside you."

My heart races faster than before, my body growing taut. I can feel it coming, the pressure building and building, and then, the pleasure. It sweeps through me, setting off bursts and sparks throughout my entire body. I cry out, feeling myself convulse around the vibrator, my eyes squeezing shut.

"Who do you belong to?" he asks, his voice slightly strained as though he's out of breath.

I don't think, surprising myself as the answer naturally flies out of my mouth as though I've said it a million times before. "You."

"Tell me," he demands. "I want to hear you say it."

My voice is a little more than a shaky breath as I say, "I belong to you."

"Good answer, baby girl," he says, sounding pleased. "You know you're my number one bitch, right?"

I blink. Did he just call me a bitch? I laugh awkwardly. "I don't know how to feel about that."

"I swear, beautiful," he says, amused, "it's a good thing."

"Okay," I say, grinning into the phone. "But I just have one question for you."

"Shoot."

"Who's your number two bitch?"

My question makes him laugh—hard. "There's no one else but you. Pick a date, baby. I really want to see you."

"Okay."

When the call ends, I'm smiling again. Smiling and excited and I shoot off a text to Richard.

ME: I'd like to go to Pennsylvania to meet Joshua. I'll let you know when.

9

What's In Your Toy Box?

———————

My cellphone pings for the second time. Sighing, I set down the ten-pound dumbbells and pick up the phone from the windowsill, taking a look. It's a text from Richard.

RICHARD: I got your message and I've been thinking ... You should go to Pennsylvania and meet your convict in person. I bet meeting him in person will get him out of your system.

He wants me to go to Pennsylvania?
I blink at the screen, confused, not sure how to respond.

———————

I'm too exhausted, too distracted by my shaky, burning legs to really comprehend the message.

"Babe, put that phone down," Becca grunts, and my eyes fly to her as she squats for what has to be the hundredth time. She's a goddamn squatting machine, holding nearly triple the weight as me, and barely breaking out in a sweat. "We're almost done. If you break too long, I swear I'll make you start again."

Groaning, I shake my head. "I'm pretty sure if I squat one more time, I won't come back up."

"Don't be so dramatic." She laughs. "You've got this, now put the phone down and pick up those weights."

My phone buzzes again. I frown as a new message pops up on the screen, another text from Richard.

RICHARD: If nothing else, I'm certain that once he sees you in person, you'll be out of his system. You should book a hotel.

I read the message, and then I read it again.

Once he sees you in person ...

My chest tightens, and so does my grip on the phone. *Asshole.* I've been working so hard—so goddamn hard—to lose weight, and I have. I've lost a ton of it, trying to make him see me as beautiful again, and he still doesn't see it.

He probably never will.

I'm not really sure he ever did.

I don't even know why I bother trying anymore, a habit I guess. And maybe, just maybe I want him to see me, really see me just once before I walk out the door.

Weights clatter to the floor behind me, and then Becca is there, her chin on my shoulder and sweaty chest against my back, peeking at my phone.

"Damn it, Becca," I say, shrugging her chin off my shoulder. "Get your nasty sweat covered body away from me."

She laughs and wraps her arms around my waist, hugging me tight. "Not until you pick up those ..." her voice trails off, her laughter abruptly stopping. "He's a horse's ass."

I turn my head to see her expression. She's frowning, long lines wrinkling her forehead, her eyes glued to my phone.

"Yeah," I agree, "he kind of is."

Silence falls.

Five, ten, fifteen seconds pass.

"Uh, Becca?" My voice is shaky, my eyes stinging.

Her arms tighten around me. "Yeah, babe?"

I glance away from her, my eyes scanning over the thousands of dollars' worth of exercise equipment filling my basement. Treadmill, elliptical, stair climber. There's a weight bench, dumbbells, and curling and deadlift bars. Yoga and pilates mats fill a quarter of the room. I bought it all, setting up a full service home gym and busting my ass daily for months, just to make Richard happy.

"Do I really look that bad?" I ask.

"Oh, honey, of course not. You look amazing."

"I'm overweight."

"You've lost thirty-two pounds."

"I need to lose another forty."

Becca snorts. "No you don't."

"The medical charts say I should be one-hundred and thirty pounds, and Richard thinks ..."

"Who gives a shit what Richard thinks," she says, cutting me off, and squeezing me tighter still. "You've got nice thick thighs, a big round butt. And your boobs are the perfect size, big enough to be noticed, but not so big they take away from those sexy eyes and full lips. You're gorgeous."

Taking a deep calming breath, I wiggle out of her arms, setting my phone back down, and I pick up my weights. "Forty-three more, right?"

Becca doesn't answer my question; instead, she gives me a look that's both fury and sadness. "Today, I'm going to make you feel sexy," she declares, her voice hinting at the emotions painting her face. "Promise."

****

When Becca said she was going to make me feel sexy, I never imagined this was what she had in mind. But as I stand here, staring at the walls of vibrators and dildos, I realize that she wasn't kidding around. She's going to make me feel sexy and she brought me to a sex toy store to do it.

I don't know how to react, standing here in skinny jeans and a bright pink spaghetti strapped tank, my eyes taking in all the toys. I'd rather be anywhere but here. They make me feel overwhelmed and a little on edge. The truth is, I've only ever been to one of these stores once before, and I didn't dawdle, picking up the first vibrator I saw, paid, and got out.

I turn, spotting Becca across the store, sorting through racks of costumes. She waves a hand, beckoning me over, but I'm not about to go to her. If I do, I'm pretty sure she'll have me trying on that sexy nurse's outfit she's holding up. By the look of it, there's no way I'd get that skirt over my ass.

When I turn back to the wall of toys, a woman is standing there. Short and blonde, with big hips and a tiny waist, wearing a light blue lacey miniskirt that just covers her ass, a skintight white tee, and flip-flops. She's smiling at me, a smile that's so warm and contagious that I find myself smiling back.

"What's in your toy box?" she asks, her voice all smooth and silky.

My toy box?

My smile falters. I don't know how to answer that. "Um … what?"

"Your toy box," she says, smiling as she waves a hand toward a display of purple vibrators. "What's in it?"

"Oh …" I stall, heat rushing to my cheeks as it dawns on me what exactly she's asking. I duck my head, glancing down. "I don't really have one."

She stares at me.

And stares at me.

And then, she stares some more.

"You don't have a vibrator or a dildo or an anal plug or a …"

My skin flares with heat as I hold up a hand, stopping her short. "I have a beaded vibrator and a bullet."

"That's it?" she asks, surprised. "Really?"

My cheeks heat further. "Yes, really."

"She's been missing out, Stacey," Becca calls, the laughter in her voice carrying from across the store. "I'm thinking she needs some anal toys and that new vibrator. You know, the one with the triple tongues?"

Anal toys?

Triple tongues?

Oh God.

"You got it, Becs." The blonde—Stacey—giggles, excited, as she grabs a hold of my arm and leads me over to the purple display. She grabs a vibrator, turning it on and grinning at me. "You're going to love this one, sweetie."

Awkwardly, I take the vibrator, feeling the powerful vibrations against my hand. My eyes widen in surprise. "Wow."

"I know, right?" she says. "And check out the clitoris

stimulator, see the tongues? They all move individually, no matter the speed setting."

Holy crap, triple tongues!

Before I know what's happening, Stacey snags up a basket and pulls me from wall to wall, display to display, filling it with more toys than I know what to do with. There's vibrators, dildos, an egg, beads, and plugs. She even adds in a panty vibrator, before moving on to the lubes and toy cleaners.

It's probably only been a few minutes, but it feels like an eternity before Becca makes her way over, smiling. She picks up a bottle of cleaner and a package of wipes, tossing them into the basket and surveying the contents, nodding approvingly. "Nice choices," she says to me, before turning to Stacey. "I'm going to steal her now."

Stacey smiles politely, gathering up a few more bottles of God only knows what, before turning away, taking the loaded basket to the counter.

"This is not making me feel sexy, Becca," I hiss. "This is making me feel awkward."

"It's not supposed to." She grins, grabbing my arm and pulling me over to the fitting room, pausing right outside the door, and pushing it open. "But this will."

I glance inside the small room, gaping. Becca has accumulated over a dozen outfits she wants me to try on, ranging from costumes to corsets to see-through body stockings.

Her hand lands on the small of my back, pushing me

inside. I'm flustered, blinking a few times, as she pulls the door closed.

"Try something on," she says. "Then, come out here and let me and Stacy see it."

"Becca ..."

I start to protest, but she doesn't let me. "Vickie, trust me. You'll feel like a sex goddess when we're done."

My brows furrow. I most definitely don't think a few see through outfits are going to make me feel anything close to a sex goddess, but I humor her, stepping over to the outfits and sorting through them.

Most of them are way too revealing, but I notice that every single one will cover my belly. God love my best friend; she chose things that'll hide the spots I hate the most. I pick up the most conservative one first: the nurses outfit.

Getting to work putting it on, I struggle zipping up the back. I step out of the fitting room, wearing the costume, not bothering to look at myself in the mirror first, finding Becca standing right outside the door with her cellphone out.

"Can you zip me up, Becca?" I ask, starting to turn around so my back is to her, but she holds up her hands to stop me.

"Pull it off your shoulder a little," she says, and when I don't comply, only looking at her as though she's insane, she does it for me, tugging the white fabric down, baring my shoulder. She reaches up, pulling out my ponytail holder and mussing up my hair, and then takes two steps back, smiling. "Perfect."

And then she raises her phone and snaps a picture.

She takes a goddamn picture!

The moment she does it, I feel as though I can't catch my breath—the store is suddenly too small, the outfit too tight. I'm on the verge of panicking when Stacey walks over, looking over Becca's shoulder, checking out the picture. "Holy shit, girl, you look hot. Like smoking hot."

My brows furrow. *I do?*

I step toward them, snagging the phone out of Becca's hand, scanning over the image. My lips part. I look ... sexy ... carefree. I look ... like a sex goddess disguised as a nurse.

Becca takes her phone back, and starts snapping more pictures, making me pose, and sit, and bend over. I listen to all her commands, too stunned at the image I saw to protest.

She must take at least twenty pictures before she shoots me a wide smile. "Go try on something else."

And I do, disappearing back into the dressing room.

****

Four hours later, I'm sitting on my bed, knees pulled up to my chest, flipping through the stack of pictures Becca took of me, modeling an obscene number of costumes and lingerie, when my phone rings. Setting down the photos, I snatch it up, glancing at the screen to see Joshua's number.

Smiling, I answer it, laying down on my back as I wait out the recording and accept the call.

"Hey, beautiful," he says, as soon as the call connects. "What's good?"

I smile. "Hey, you."

"How was your day?"

His question causes an awkward laugh to spill from my lips. "It was ... interesting."

He's silent for a moment, most likely waiting for me to elaborate. When I say nothing more, he presses, "Interesting?"

"Yes," I confirm, laughing again. "Interesting."

He laughs lightly. "Are you going to fill me in, baby girl?"

"Well," I say, hesitating for a moment. "I worked out with Becca and in the middle of the workout I received a text message from Richard that made me feel like shit. Then, I went to a sex toy store, bought a crap load of toys and sexy outfits, and Becca took a crap load of sexy photos while I tried everything on."

He's silent for a beat. "What did the text message say?"

"Seriously?" I ask, giggling. "Out of everything, that's what you focus on?"

"Yeah, beautiful," he says. "What did it say?"

"It said that I should come and meet you in person, that once you see me, I'll be out of your system." My voice cracks on the words, and tears sting my eyes as I try to hold back the hurt and anger and fear that's filling me up, threatening to drown me.

The line is stone cold silent for a second before his quiet voice comes through. "What the fuck? Why would he think that?"

"Because ..." I stall, letting out another awkward laugh.

Joshua lets out a long sigh. "Don't shut down on me, baby girl. There's no need to feel awkward. Not with me. Tell me why he'd text you that bullshit?"

"I'm ..." I hesitate, not sure I want to answer that, but holding my breath, I do it anyway. "Because I'm overweight."

"You don't look overweight in your photos," he says. "You look curvy and sexy as fuck."

"Well, I am. I've lost a lot, but I still have more to go."

"How much do you weigh?" He sounds confused.

My stomach is in knots. "Does it matter?"

"Nope, just curious," he says, and his voice ... his voice sounds genuine.

The moment he says it, a smile lights up my face. "You're pretty awesome, you know that, right?"

"I think you're pretty awesome, too," he says. "So when are you coming to see me?"

"Does two weeks give you enough time to get me approved for a visit?"

"Yeah, it does."

"Okay, let me just check my calendar." Putting him on speaker phone, I tap on my calendar, pulling it up and scanning through my deadlines. "How about I come on October ninth and tenth? It's a Friday and Saturday."

"Sounds perfect," he says. "Do I get to see the sexy pictures?"

I laugh sharply, my body heating at his words. How does he do that, melting my nerves away with just a few words? "I don't think so."

"Why not?"

"Because no one's going to see them," I say on a laugh. "Ever."

"One day you'll be sending me sexy pictures, beautiful," he says confidently. "You'll be doing it because you want to, without me asking, and it'll give you a thrill doing it. I promise you that."

"I ... uh ... I ..." I'm not sure how to respond to that. I start stammering and stuttering, my face heating and flushing. Oh God, I feel like such a damn fool. I guess my nerves aren't completely gone after all.

He laughs, genuinely amused. "I fucking love how shy you are. You're perfect, you know that? All sweet and innocent. I love that about you."

"Really?" I ask disbelievingly, because I honestly can't believe someone like him would want anything to do with a shy and innocent girl like me.

"Really," he confirms, and then pauses for a beat. "Now tell me about your new toys."

10

Problem Areas and Fat Arms

I'm sweating.

Full on, shirt staining, hair soaking, sweating.

It's not pretty.

So much for this whole working out thing getting easier as time goes on. I've reverted back months to the can't catch my breath, dripping wet fat girl trying to lose weight.

I glance at my timer. Ten minutes and thirteen … no, twelve seconds to go.

Shit. My legs aren't going to make it and my ass … oh my God, my ass is on fire. Squats suck. They suck so hard.

It's a little after three o'clock in the afternoon, and I've been at my legs work-out for nearly fifty minutes. I probably shouldn't even be doing it today, not with the crazy list of things I need to get done before taking the trip to Pennsylvania tomorrow, but my nerves are shot, and I thought the work-out might calm me.

It hasn't.

With every goddamn squat I do, I add another two items to the list. Most important so far: a doctor's appointment and finding a wireless bra that will go through the metal detector at the prison.

"You're doing squats again."

The voice startles me so much that I jump, yelping, and nearly drop the dumbbells. Turning to the stairs, I see Richard standing there, his dark blonde hair mussed, dressed in track pants and a tee.

"Shit you scared me," I mumble, turning back around and adjusting my stance. "When did you get back?"

"Ten minutes ago," he says. "Don't you have packing to do?"

"Yeah." I squat down, slowly standing back up. "I'm almost done, though."

He lets out a chuckle, the sound grating. "So, you're really going to go."

"Yes, I am."

Richard strolls through the basement then, adjusts the weight bench to an inclined position, and sits down, before reaching for the forty-pound dumbbells. "When are you coming back again?"

"I'll be back Sunday."

He nods, saying nothing further as he begins a set of incline presses. He's watching me, smirking, looking as though he's trying hard not to laugh as I squat, and squat, and squat.

My timer buzzes—finally. I go to my phone, setting it for a new ten-minute session, before swapping my twenty pound dumbbells for tens, and then I lunge, and I lunge, and I lunge some more.

My workout becomes awkward. I want to jump out of my own skin. I don't know what to say, or what to do. I feel as though I barely know the man anymore. He watches me, his face expressionless. I have no idea what he's thinking, but I hate the feeling of his eyes on me while I'm working out.

It's uncomfortable.

It's unnerving.

It's ...

"Why don't you work on your problem areas like those fat arms?"

His question freezes me and my hand weights clatter to the floor as my gaze snaps to his, taking in his hard, compassionless expression as he presses out another rep.

"What did you just say?"

He merely shrugs. "You're always doing squats and lunges, but it's those arms you need to work on."

The nonchalance of his voice twists my stomach up in knots. Anger boils in my veins.

I glare at him.

And glare at him.

And then glare at him some more.

It's not Richard's fault that I'm fat. It's nobody's fault but my own that I gained the weight, that I couldn't find a healthier way to deal with the stress and depression, but that doesn't give him the right to talk to me the way he does.

"I worked on arms yesterday," I mutter eventually, somehow managing to hide the sharp pain his words cause me. "It's really not my fault you only ever show up on leg days."

He raises his eyebrows. "Some of us have to work, Vic."

A moment of silence and more anger simmers, masking the pain spreading through my chest. "It's too bad you still don't see what I do as work. Maybe if you did, maybe if you supported my career even a little, we wouldn't be where we are now."

He lets out a deep sigh. "I've always supported your writing."

I laugh once. "Oh, yeah? Name one of my books, any one of them."

More silence.

I'm dumbfounded. I don't even know what to think. Twenty-three published books and the man can't even name one. I swallow thickly, pushing down my feelings.

"That's what I thought." Carefully, I pick up the weights and place them on the rack, before picking up my phone and turning off the timer. "I've got to go. I've got a doctor's appointment."

I walk upstairs, leaving him there. I shower and dress,

somehow managing not to let the tears fall. I grab my purse from my office before I head out the door. Richard is still in the basement when I leave and I don't bother to tell him that I'm going.

Getting in the car, I glance at the clock as I start it up. I still have an hour before my appointment but not enough time to go bra shopping. So I head over to the post office, hoping there may be a new letter from Joshua, because I sure as hell could use something to smile about right now.

Sure enough, there's a letter sitting in my post box, along with a delivery slip. I head up to the counter, collecting the package, not even bothering to look at it before rushing out to my car and tearing into the letter.

October 1, 2015

Smile, you're beautiful!

Only nine more days until I finally get to see your sexy ass. I'm so fucking excited. I feel like I've known you all my life, but I can't stop thinking about the moment when I get to hold you in my arms, hug and kiss you. It's going to be epic, I can feel it.

So what are you thinking about, my beautiful angel? Me? Well, I'm thinking about you. I'm always thinking about you, twenty-four-seven. I was in a pretty dark place when you started writing me, but you've made my life brighter. I don't think you really get this, but you truly are an angel to me. You've made me happy even while I'm stuck behind these fences. You've brought light back into my world, and I'm so fucking thankful for that.

Please know that I see you for you, I appreciate you for you, and I'm never letting you go.

I hope that doesn't freak you out, if it does, I'm sorry, but it's true. You're too precious to let slip away.

So I'm really hoping I timed this letter right. If I did, then today you should have also received a package from my parents. I hope you don't mind that I gave them your address. It was just a lot easier to have them send the present I had made for you and fill out all those customs forms. Mailing stuff to Canada is harder than I thought it would be.

Anyway, did you get the teddy bear I had made for you? I hope you did and you like it. One of the guys here makes them. The JV on the chest is for me and you, and the guy who made it said he made a little backpack for it with a heart on it. I didn't get to see it before it was mailed. Could you send me a picture of you with it?

I was talking about you with my mom today. I talk about you a lot. She said she noticed a difference in me since I started talking to you. Have you noticed it? She said I'm calmer. I feel calmer. It's your voice, I think. It's soothing.

I wonder what it's going to be like when we kiss for the first time. I think it'll be electric, but I'm nervous to be honest. I haven't kissed a woman in years, and I'm not sure if I'm going to be good at it anymore. What about you? Are you nervous?

I can't believe we've only been writing and talking for a little over three months now. Some days it feels like I've always known you. I wish I could talk to you right now, but you're busy editing your next book. I'm so fucking excited to read this one. I can't wait for you to send me a copy. Can I get the very first one? I think that would be so cool to have the first printed copy. If not, no worries. Just thought it couldn't hurt to ask.

Did I tell you my sister is prego? I'm so excited for her. It'll be her third kid. Sucks that I won't get to be there when it's born, though. Still, it's exciting.

Well, it's lunch time here, so I've got to go. Know that you are beautiful and smart and sexy, and I'm so fucking grateful to have you in my life. I can't wait to finally meet you even though it feels like I've known you all my life.

Yours always,
Joshua

Carefully, I fold the letter, placing it back in the envelope, before turning to the box. I try to open it, but there's so much tape keeping it closed that I end up having to stab it with my keys a few times before I make any headway.

And then—finally—I get the box open.

I tear into it, excited to see the teddy bear. Pulling it out, I let out a little gasping squeal. It's purple. *Purple.* The bear is knitted, made with a soft wool. So cool. I can't believe another inmate actually made it.

And it's the most adorable thing I've ever seen, and Jesus, that tiny backpack is awesome.

I'm not sure how long I stare at it, checking out the details in the stitching, when I remember about my appointment. Reluctantly, I put the bear back into the box, and start up my car.

I go to the doctor, refill my birth control pills, and then I head to the mall, on the hunt for a wireless bra, which is a surprisingly challenging task. It takes me three stores and at least twenty bras before I finally find one that's somewhat comfortable. I'm in the fitting room, about to take the bra off, when my phone rings.

Pulling it out of my purse, I glance at the screen.

Joshua.

I answer it, accepting the call.

"My beautiful angel," he says, his voice, light and happy. "I can't wait to see you. Only two more days."

"Hey, you," I say, forcing a smile, my mind—unfortunately—still on my fat arms. "Thank you so much for the bear and letter. I love them both, so freakin' much."

"I'm glad you like them." He's silent for a moment. "You okay, baby girl? Your voice sounds a little off."

"I fucking hate him," I say right away. "He's such a dick."

I don't know what it is about hearing Joshua's voice that makes me suddenly feel like the flood gates are about to open, but it does. Maybe it's because I know he cares, or perhaps it's that I know he'll make me feel better if I do cry.

Joshua sighs. "I take it your husband's home early."

"Yes," I say, my voice cracking on the word as I try damn hard to hold back the threatening tears. I sit down on the changing room stool, wrapping an arm around my belly.

"Are you crying?"

"No, I'm fine."

"Baby," he says, his voice turning soft. "Tell me what happened."

I sniffle. It's stupid, I know. I feel ridiculous crying over this, but there's just something about Joshua, something that makes me feel so comfortable and safe, that all my worries and stresses just pour out. Even so, I wipe away the tears, trying to pull myself together. "It's nothing, really ... I'm overreacting. He just makes me so mad. I swear he knows exactly what to say to hurt me."

Joshua lets out another long sigh. "What did he say to you, baby?"

"I was doing squats and lunges and he said I should work on my problem areas, like my fat arms."

"Fucking dick."

Silence falls.

I sniffle again, my mind falling to Richard, to his text messages and insinuations. What if he's right about the fat thing? What if Joshua sees me and wants nothing more to do with me? He's seen pictures, he knows I'm a curvy girl, but every single picture I've sent him over the last couple of months has been ... only the most flattering angles.

"There's something else," I say, my stomach twisting up. "Something I want to tell you."

"Okay."

"You asked about my weight."

"Baby, it doesn't matter."

"Just let me get this out, okay?" I pause, taking a breath. "I'm one-hundred and eighty-four pounds. I've lost a little over thirty pounds in the last six months, but my weight loss has kind of stopped. No matter what I do or how many hours a day I spend working out, I just stay the same."

The words pour out of me, tears stinging in my eyes once more as bile burns in my throat. This is it. This is the moment he's going to tell me I'm not good enough.

This is the moment when Richard's horrible words become reality.

Suddenly, I'm kicking myself for not telling Joshua my fat status from the start. I would have confessed it in the first letter if I'd known it would save me this much heartache.

"That's it?" he asks.

My brow furrows. "Yeah."

"It's no big deal," he says. "Weight's something that can be changed. We'll work on it together."

"Really?"

"Really," he confirms. "I'll tell you what. I'll spend some time this weekend and put together some workouts for you. It's really no big deal. I've been working out my whole life so it won't take me long to put something together for you."

I roll my eyes, laughing a little, stunned. He sounds so goddamn relaxed about this. I wish I had even an ounce of his confidence. "Thank you."

"It'll all work out," he says, reassuringly. "Just think,

tomorrow at this time you'll be on your way up here and you'll get some time away from him. Time to clear your head and relax."

I smile, my voice turning soft as I say, "I can't wait."

11

Metal Detectors and Wireless Bras

The metal detector beeps.

"Step back through and take off your shoes, ma'am," the guard says. "Do you have any other metal on you, jewelry or your bra?"

"No, sir," I say, my voice squeaking on the words. Shit, I'm nervous. My hands are shaking as I unzip my knee-high boots. "No jewelry other than what's already in the dish and my bra is wireless."

He nods as I place the boots on the counter, watching as another guard begins to search them, running a gloved hand inside, feeling along the interior.

"Try again," the first guard says, waving me through the detector once more.

I step through cautiously, careful not to touch the side, but the damn thing beeps again.

My stomach twists into painfully tight knots. That was twice. *Twice.* I only have one more shot at this before he won't let me in.

"I'm sorry," I say, lifting my shoulders helplessly. "I don't know what's setting it off."

"You're okay. We'll get you through," he says, cracking a small, reassuring smile. He points toward a box of clear plastic bags at the end of the counter. "Why don't you take one of those bags, go to the bathroom and put your bra inside. It could be the clasps on the back setting it off. You'll be able to put it back on once it's inspected."

"Okay, sure." I offer him a smile, trying to get my shaking hands under control as I step over to the bags, taking a deep breath as I reach in and grab one.

It doesn't take me long to get out of my bra, and within moments, I'm back at the counter with it in hand. I feel my body flush as I set it on the counter. I know my nervousness is written all over my face. I cross my arms over my chest, attempting to give some support to my breasts as I try hard to ignore the guard patting down my bra.

The other guard meets my eyes, his green ones bright and smiling, and he nods me through the metal detector once again.

I hold my breath as I step through, praying the issue was the bra.

I laugh awkwardly. "I guess all that time I spent looking for a wireless bra was a waste of time."

He laughs at that, a deep, soothing sound, as he picks up a stamp, dabbing it against the ink pad. "Guess so. Your right hand, please."

Holding out my hand, he stamps it. It's clear, nothing showing up on my skin, and for a moment I wonder what it's for. He must see the question on my face because he smiles again and says, "It's a black light stamp. When you leave, a guard will check to make sure you've got it under a black light."

"Oh, okay." I pick up my bra. "Do I go back to the bathroom to put this on?"

"You can step into that room right there to put your bra back on, ma'am," he says, pointing to a door behind me. "When you come out, you're going to go through this door, and follow the yellow painted walkway. It'll lead you right up to the visiting area."

"Thank you," I say, picking up all my belongings, turning away and stepping into the small room.

Closing the door behind me, I try to lock it, but the lock doesn't work, not that I'm surprised. The room looks like a strip search area—a table in the corner and a small blue pail filled with a bunch of plastic bra bags.

Quickly, I lift up my snug fitting purple sweater dress, putting on my bra and fastening it, and then I smooth my dress back in place. I pull my boots on, zipping them up, and then I fasten the bracelet Joshua made for me before stepping out of the room and through the doors.

It's at that moment that I notice the fences.

Walking through the door, I see the tall, barbed wire fences looming in front and surrounding me. I have no choice but to walk forward, stopping at a gate. I try to open it, but it won't budge—locked. I'm about to turn around when I hear the mechanical grinding of the lock popping open, so I reach for it again, stepping into a small, wire enclosure—with another gate.

I step up to it and wait.

And wait.

And wait.

It feels as though ten minutes pass before the lock pops open and I can finally pass through, though I'm sure it's only seconds, and then, I'm following the yellow painted walkway.

It's not a far walk, only a few minutes and a set of stairs to get to the visiting area. I walk in, glancing around nervously, feeling severely self-conscious as I pass by a line of vending machines and step up to the next desk, smiling at yet another guard.

"Who are you here to see?" he asks, not looking up from his computer screen.

"Joshua Larson."

"Go to table 25." He points toward the back of the room. "Straight down this aisle, second last one at the end."

"May I get snacks first?" I ask nervously, not really sure if I'm allowed to.

He looks up at me then, smiling a little. "Sure. Your inmate will be here shortly."

"Thank you," I say, turning back to the vending machines. It takes seconds to find the drink and Swedish Fish that Joshua had asked for. I grab the snacks and make my way to the table, taking a seat.

And then I wait.

Inmates come in.

Visitors get snacks.

Inmates leave.

And I wait, my eyes glued to the glass enclosed room that the inmates seem to be coming and going from.

Minutes pass. One, five, eight.

I'm getting restless, my knees jumping, bumping against the knee high table. My hands are fidgeting, constantly running along my dress, smoothing it out, and my mind is racing trying to remember all the rules. No more than a ten-second hug and kiss at the beginning and end of the visit. Holding hands is permitted as long as your hands are above the table and visible to the guard. Inmates are not allowed to touch money or use vending ...

And then I see him.

Joshua steps into the glass room, dressed in all green, his eyes scanning the visitors area as he waits for a guard. When his gaze lands on mine, he smiles widely and waves—yes, he waves—looking like an excited child.

It feels like an eternity passes as he's patted down by a guard and checks in at the desk, but then everything seems to happen too fast, and suddenly he's standing at our table, smiling down at me.

"You look beautiful," he says, stopping at our table, still smiling as he hangs his coat on the back of his plastic chair. Holding a hand out to me, he says, "Come here, sexy."

"Hey you," I say, standing up. I'm shaking, trembling, as he pulls me into his arms. He yanks me to him quickly, so close that I can feel every bit of his hard sculpted body pressed against me. Feeling those hard muscles makes me all too aware of my own generous curves. My chest feels as though it's about to explode, my heart thumping so hard it nearly hurts. And then he pulls me closer still, his grip so tight that I know I'll never be able to wiggle my way out, not unless he allows it, and I abso-freakin'-lutely love it.

Best embrace ever.

His lips work over mine, his tongue filling my mouth as soon as our lips touch. There's nothing gentle about it. He claims my lips with the same force he used to pull me to him.

The kiss ends too soon, though it's not by choice. *Stupid ten second rule.* I want to lean into him again, feel those soft lips of his against mine just one more time, but he steps away, letting me go just as abruptly as he pulled me in, and takes a seat.

Unbelievably, I'm shakier now than I was before the

kiss. I wobble back to my chair, taking an embarrassingly ungraceful seat. I look at him. "That was ... wow."

My words make him laugh. "Yeah, baby, it was *wow*."

Silence falls.

It's not pleasant.

It's awkward and long and I want to break it, but dammit if I'm not tongue-tied and speechless. I glance around, scoping out the other tables. They're nearly all full, inmates and their loved ones smiling and chatting. Everyone seems so relaxed. Even the guards are chatting with each other, barely looking in anyone's direction.

It's ... odd and seriously not what I was expecting.

Joshua raises his eyebrows, looking at me peculiarly, as he reaches for the packet of Swedish Fish, popping one into his mouth. "Baby, why are you shaking?"

I'm so embarrassed I can feel my face heating. What's wrong with me, shaking like a goddamn leaf? I want to slink away, go hide over by the vending machines. "Just ignore me. My hands always shake a little. Tremors, they run in my family."

He laughs. "It's your whole body, sweetness. Are you nervous?"

"Little bit. Is it that obvious?"

"Yeah," he says, laughing again. "It is."

I stare at him, taking him in. Jesus, he looks even better in person. I can see some of his tattoos. The devil and dragons on his forearms. They're sexy as hell.

Silence lingers between us as he pops another candy

into his mouth, watching me intently. I want to say something—anything—but I have no words. I can't believe I'm here. I can't believe he's here. I ...

"You want to play a game?"

A game?

No, not really. I'm too nervous to concentrate. "Um, sure."

A legitimate look of surprise crosses his face, but he wipes it away quickly, smiling once more. I guess he wasn't expecting me to say yes. "How about Scrabble?"

No, anything but Scrabble. I suck at Scrabble.

I smile. "Sounds good."

He stands up and walks away from the table, heading over to a desk behind us that I hadn't noticed before. He smiles and chats with the guard there for a moment, before picking up the board game and making his way back to our table.

He's quiet as he opens the box, laying the board and shaking up the playing pieces. Once he's done, he glances up at me, smiling as he opens the bag for me. "Pick your tiles."

We play in silence for a while, and each time he picks up his drink, taking a sip, I kick myself for not grabbing one for myself. My throat is dry, so is my mouth, nerves wreaking havoc on my body. I lick my lips, still tasting the cinnamon taste from his kiss. I bet he ate one of those fireball candies he likes so much before coming up to the visit.

I lay down a word, and so does he, his, triple the length of my measly three letters. And the silence continues.

Shit. What are we going to do for five hours if we can't even talk for five minutes in person?

"So talk to me, baby girl," he says eventually, studying his pieces. "Tell me something new about yourself."

"Hmmm ... let's see," I say, stalling, trying hard not to think about how hard he's staring at me, taking in every detail as though there just might be a test later. I'm pretty sure if there is, he'd ace it. "Okay, a story. Did I ever tell you about the time one of my horses decided to help unpack the groceries?"

He shakes his head. "No, but I'd like to hear it."

"Okay," I say, my eyes falling back to the tiles, searching for a word. "It was wintertime and Pepper had gotten out of the fence. He did that a lot, always finding the weak points to break through. Anyway, we were unloading the groceries, and the horse came up checking things out. I grabbed a bag full of bread and a case of soda from the trunk, and he followed me right into the house, yanking a loaf of bread out of the bag as I set it down, and took back off out of the house. It took me and my sisters thirty minutes of chasing him around the property before we managed to get the loaf of bread back."

Joshua leans back in his chair, and chuckles. "I can't believe he fit through the door."

"Mom was so angry," I tell him, laughing as I lay down

another three-letter word. "She'd just painted the hardwood floors and he scratched them all up."

"I bet." He laughs again. "I'd be pissed, too."

We play seven rounds of Scrabble and the man kicks my ass every time. I seem to be the master of three-letter words.

I make him a vending machine hamburger. Gross. But he assures me that it's like gourmet food compared to what they get at mealtimes. He tries to get me to eat with him, but I settle for just a Diet Coke, not sure I want to risk the vending machines.

And we talk—a lot.

At some point, the time stops slugging by, flying instead. Hours feel like minutes; minutes feel like seconds. My hands stop shaking, my heart stops racing, although those butterflies in my belly never do take a rest.

I don't want the visit to end—ever. But looking at the clock, I know that we don't have much longer. Fifteen, maybe twenty minutes left.

"Are you having fun?" he asks, still watching me as intently as when he first sat down. I'm too focused on making a word that's more than three letters to let the attention bother me anymore.

"Yes, are you?" I ask, lifting my eyes to his.

He nods, chuckling. "I've got to tell you, baby, I thought you'd be better at Scrabble than you are."

I let out a sharp laugh. "Are you saying I suck at Scrabble?"

"You don't suck," he responds, his voice teasing, as he picks up his bottled drink and takes a sip. "You're just not as good as I thought you'd be, being an author and all."

"I depend on spell check a lot," I mutter, and it's true. "I've actually mastered how to spell inconvenience wrong enough for spell check to understand it."

"Seriously?" he asks, eyes widening. "Wouldn't it make more sense to learn how to spell it right?"

I shrug a shoulder. "You'd think, but my brain always wants to add a 't'."

I'm quiet for a moment as a guard appears at our table, letting us know that our time is almost up, before walking away.

I take a sip of my soda. "This sucks. I can't believe it's already over."

He smiles softly. "We get five more hours tomorrow, beautiful, and a lot more Scrabble to come."

There's something refreshing about the way he looks at it—instead of being upset, he smiles, looking forward to the next good thing. I could learn a lot from his outlook.

"Yeah," I say. "You're right."

"You might want to brush up on your spelling skills," he continues. "It's almost sad how badly I destroyed you at the game given your profession."

I slouch back in my chair, taking another sip of my drink. "Right, I'll study the dictionary tonight."

Joshua chuckles and leans over the table, closer to me,

taking my hands in his, rubbing them. "Want to know a secret?"

"Yes."

"I've been practicing with some of the guys since you said you were coming," he says, and I swear there's a little red in his cheeks suddenly. "I thought you'd like this game because you're an author and I didn't want to look bad playing against you."

I laugh once, surprised. "Seriously?"

"Seriously," he says, nodding, and then his expression turns serious. "Before you go, I've got something important to tell you, but I wanted to tell you this in person."

I laugh timidly, biting my bottom lip. "Okay ..."

He stares at me, his eyes surveying my face as his expression turns serious, his voice dropping low. "Through our letters and phone calls, I feel we've created an amazing connection, one I've never felt before. I wanted to wait until we were face to face and after we kissed to make sure I was one-hundred percent correct about my feelings. You're the woman of my dreams, and I've fallen head over heels in love with you."

My breath hitches. "You have?"

"Yeah, I have," he says, watching me tentatively. "I don't want you to feel any pressure to have to say it back to me. I want you to mean it when you say it. This is just something that I couldn't keep inside anymore."

Joshua is watching me curiously and I don't know what

to say. My face flushes. I don't know if I'm mad at him for waiting until the end of the visit to tell me this, or happy about it.

Maybe both.

I'm really not sure.

He stands up then, pulling me up with him, tugging me back into his arms. I stumble, catching myself on his chest, my arms instinctively wrapping around his neck.

Cupping the back of my neck with the perfect amount of pressure, he tilts my head so I have no choice but to look up at him. His thumb sweeps across my bottom lip, and I let out a shuddering breath as he tilts his head, and his lips hit mine.

He seizes me then, pulling me in tight, one of his hands digging into the small of my back, while the other puts more pressure on the back of my head. There's no gentleness to the kiss, no sign of the tenderness he typically shows me.

The man kisses me like he means it, like he needs it, like he's never going to let me go.

I don't want him to let me go.

When he pulls away, I let out a sound that I've never heard come from my lips before. It's a whimper or a moan or perhaps it's a mix of both, and a hint of a smile takes over his face when he hears it.

"Love you, beautiful," he says, his thumb taking one more quick pass across my bottom lip. "I'll see you tomorrow."

12

L Word Awkwardness

I'm a mess, nervous and tired, only half-dressed, wearing leggings and a hot pink bra and trying to put on my makeup.

It's not going well.

My hands are shaky, causing my eyeliner to jiggle across my lids. Groaning, I set the pencil down and reach for the makeup remover, glancing at the clock.

It's just after one o'clock in the afternoon.

That means I have an hour and a half to torture myself and try to convince myself that this is real, that Joshua meant what he said and he isn't just playing me—using me.

And torture myself, I do. I try to figure out what to do,

what to think, replaying every word Joshua said at the end of the visit yesterday.

When I finally manage to get my eyeliner on straight, I finish getting ready, straightening my hair, and then stressing over my clothes, before settling on a pair of dark wash skinny jeans and a black empire-style top, finishing off my look with a pair of black knee-high boots.

And then I pace around my hotel room, continually glancing at the clock, not wanting to arrive at the prison too early, but also not wanting to be late. By the time two o'clock arrives, I'm a frazzled bundle of nerves, convinced that the man is just messing with me.

Swallowing down a wave of unease, I make sure to grab my room key, stuffing it in my purse as I head out the door.

My heart races as I drive to the prison, nearly missing each and every turn. I have to remove my bra again to get through the metal detector, along with my boots, but it's not nearly as scary this time.

I'm sitting at our table with my head down, Joshua's drink and Swedish Fish waiting for him, when he appears beside me, taking off his coat and placing it over the back of his chair.

I blink a few times, too lost in my own head to notice his approach. "Uh, hey."

"Hey, beautiful," he says, grinning as he takes a step toward me. "Come here."

Standing up, I take a small, hesitant step toward him. I guess I'm not moving fast enough because suddenly, he's on me. His arms wrapping around my waist, his fingers digging into my lower back.

And then those beautiful, kissable lips hit mine.

My insides warm and my knees shake. His lips push mine open, hungry. He tastes like cinnamon again, and although I don't really care for cinnamon, on him, I love it. Can't get enough of it.

My own hunger unleashes as his tongue rubs against mine, causing my pulse to jump in excitement and my nipples to peak. I wrap my arms around his neck, pulling him closer, completely forgetting about the guards and inmates close by.

I forget everything.

Forget my anger.

Forget my anxiety and conflict.

For those ten seconds, I forget everything but him.

Joshua pulls away, laughing softly against my lips. "Missed you, gorgeous."

The words and the unmistakable arousal in his voice send my heart crashing into my rib cage. I whisper, "I missed you, too."

His arms drop from my waist then, and reluctantly, I let my arms fall from his neck, both of us taking a seat. We sit in silence for a moment, my anxiety ramping back up as Joshua rips into his candy, popping one into his mouth, grinning as he chews it. "How was the hotel? Did you sleep alright?"

"Sure," I say, shrugging. "The hotel was great."

He looks at me, and then his mouth opens for a moment before anything actually comes out. "You look tired."

That's because I am tired.

And confused.

And annoyed.

Joshua reaches across, taking my hand and rubbing it, his eyes hot, but yet, concerned. "What's wrong?"

Everything.

I look at him, feeling slightly high and dizzy. He's cute. No, scratch that. He's sexy. He's hot. He's ... perfect. Not just looks perfect, but inside, too. He's sweet, thoughtful, caring. He's just ... perfect, and yet, I can't rid myself of the anger that's been simmering in my veins since yesterday's visit.

"Nothing's wrong," I mutter, squeezing his hand, and hope to hell that I sound nonchalant enough. "Just bummed that it's the last visit, I guess."

I can't miss his sudden amused smile. He shakes his head, chuckling softly. "Baby, I can tell something's wrong. Just tell me what's going on."

Smiling in return, hoping to ease the blow, I pull my hands away, leaning back in my chair. "I think you're an ass."

"Baby, why would you say something like that?" he whispers sadly, his grin vanishing.

I lift an eyebrow. "Because you are. How could you tell me you love me just before the visit ended? Totally uncool."

We stare at each other.

And then we stare some more.

Finally, he whispers, "Beautiful, I just couldn't keep it in anymore. I'm madly in love with you and I needed to tell you." He pauses for a moment, glancing around the packed visitation room. "I didn't know what your reaction would be so I waited until the end of the visit so you wouldn't give me a bad reaction. I didn't want you to feel forced, like you had to say it back or have an awkward moment, so I just waited until the end."

I stare at him again, tempted to just let it go and pretend everything's good.

But I can't.

I want to.

But I can't.

"And this isn't awkward now?" I ask.

"I think you're kind of making it awkward, baby. I think you should be happy that I expressed how much I love you, how much I want to be with you."

His voice has a hint of anger in it, bitterness that makes my stomach twist into knots.

"You didn't even call," I accuse. "You didn't give me the chance to talk to you about it."

"Baby." He reaches out to take my hand within his, his eyes never leaving mine as he begins to rub it. "I couldn't get a chance to call you. The phones were packed. If I could have called you, I would have. You know that."

"Stop calling me baby," I whisper. "Please."

God, I just need him to stop. Stop being so sweet and nice. I'm defenseless against the way he speaks to me and the words he uses. I've always wanted someone to talk to me like this. I've *dreamed* about it.

But now that I have it, I don't know what to do with it, how to react.

Where's the tough biker? The murderer?

He laughs, giving me a look that makes my heart melt a little. It's hot, but yet sweet, his brown eyes staring right into my mind ... my heart. "Come on, Victoria," he says. "You know you love it when I call you baby and beautiful."

My cheeks blaze red.

He's right. I do.

I like it too much, I think, and I hate that he knows that. Knows it's what I need.

"I'm married." I blurt the words out like vomit, uncontrolled and unwanted. My cheeks flare with heat. What's wrong with me?

He rolls his eyes at me. "Beautiful, I already know that, and I also know you're going to leave your husband. You love me, you just have a hard time telling me this. I can see it in your eyes."

Really? Am I really that obvious?

"You can?"

"Yes, baby girl, I can tell you love me."

I sigh, looking down at our hands clasped together, loving the way it feels to have his big ones wrapped around my smaller ones. I love the contact, crave it, actually. It's been so long since a man did something as simple as hold my hand and it feels ... good.

Too good.

I look back up at him, meeting his eyes. "How?"

His eyes study me for a beat before he responds, an odd smile pulling at his lips. "By the way you kiss me and look at me. By the way you shake just when I hold you in my arms."

Silence falls.

Long silence.

Awkward silence.

Joshua massages my hands, waiting patiently. I can't tell him that every day of my life I've tried to picture someone like him in my life.

I sigh. "I think I do love you."

"Aw, beautiful." He smiles, a panty-melting smile. "I already know."

"It scares me. It terrifies me."

And it's true. Fear pulses through me like a living organism. Every word that leaves his mouth gnaws away at my confidence, making me doubt everything.

"Why?" he asks. "Why be afraid of love?"

I shake my head. "You don't fit into my life."

"Baby, I realize that I'm in a bad place. I know I'm in prison, but you came into my life for a reason, you were drawn to me for a reason. This was meant to be. It was destiny, us crossing each other's paths. Maybe this isn't the picture perfect lifestyle you were looking for, but I promise we will have a good life together. Just give me a chance."

I smile, and he looks at me, giving me a sexy *almost* smile, and just like that, I feel it—really feel it. The flutter of happiness. The glimpse of what I could have if I just took the leap.

"Can you picture yourself living in a cookie-cutter house, with a minivan and a kid, and a career? Not getting into trouble, not going back to the bikers."

"Baby," he says, drawing the word out as a smirk plays on his lips. "I'm always going to be a biker. It's something you're going to have to understand and accept, but could I see myself creating a family with you?" He smiles brightly. "Of course, baby. I really am in love with you. I've always wanted a family."

My heart picks up speed and a flicker of alarm passes through me. I try to sit up straight, pulling my hands away, but his grip tightens, holding me fast.

"You mean you're really considering going back to all of that?" I ask. "After spending eight years in prison because you were wearing your colors, you would go back to that ... that life?"

"Yes," he says simply. "I plan on going back to that after my four years of paper are done. It's a lifestyle."

I snort. "Yeah, I've seen how that lifestyle plays out for women. I watched *Sons of Anarchy*. I know how it ends for those women."

"Baby," he sighs, lips flattening into a thin line as he

scrubs at his face as though he's in for a headache. "You're watching a TV show that glorifies certain aspects of the biker lifestyle, but half of that is for TV so people will watch it. You don't even have a clue what any of it means or what it is."

"Glorified? Both the main women die."

"Well, Victoria," he says, a flash of amusement passing across his eyes. "I've been in prison so I haven't actually seen the last few seasons so I really don't know that, but please don't ruin the show for me."

"Sorry," I mutter, dropping my eyes.

"It's okay." Joshua reaches a hand out, placing a finger under my chin, forcing my eyes back up to his. When he continues, his voice is soft, reassuring. "It'll be years before I can get back into the life. I've got four years of paper when I get out. I'm not going to do something stupid where it would bring me back to prison for another four years."

"What does four years of paper mean?"

"I have four years of parole, my love. I can't have anything to do with motorcycle clubs, can't go to bars. So don't worry your pretty little heart. It'll be a long time before any of this matters, and who knows, maybe I'll change my mind by then."

I know he's lying; know he's just trying to reassure me. He wants me to think there's a chance he won't go back to the club life. I can see it in his eyes, hear it in his voice.

I want him to tell me the truth, that he's set on going back. I don't want to play games. Not with him.

Even so, I force myself to nod and smile, reminding myself that it's seven and a half years away. Tons of time to change his mind.

I want to ask him about it, but by the smirk on his face, I know he already knows what I'm thinking. Instead, I glance toward the guards' desk and say, "I think we should play some cards."

He laughs. "Ooo, changing the subject, are we?"

I blink innocently and smile. "Maybe."

"I think that's a great idea and I think we should keep score because I bet I'll win."

A laugh bubbles out of me. "You won't win. I will kick your ass."

"Oh, yeah, beautiful?" he says, that sexy smile returning to his face. "Why don't you go get a deck of cards from the guards' desk and show me?"

Pushing back my chair, I stand up, grinning down at him. "Oh, I will." And as I walk toward the guards' desk, I find myself feeling a little less confused.

13

Talk Dirty To Me

I feel ... high.

I'm floating. With each breath I take, butterflies dance in my stomach. It's a peaceful feeling, warm and relaxed.

Stalling my footsteps, I glance back at Joshua. He's watching me, his lips curving with a smile as he waves goodbye to me. He mouths 'I love you', before turning away, following the guard to the glass room, ready to be pat down.

A genuine smile lights up my face as I turn back around and walk again. A kiss, a touch, a single smile from that man does more than any drug, any drink ever could do for me.

I take a deep breath as soon as I'm out on the pathway leading to the prison exit. The evening air is so cold my skin prickles with goosebumps. It's not too late, only six-thirty, but it's already dark.

I walk quickly, following the yellow painted pathway. It only takes me a few minutes to reach the gate. I stick my right hand through the opening just before the gate, allowing a guard to see my black light stamp, and then I wait for the gate to unlock.

The guards in the reception area eye me as I step toward my locker, retrieving my purse and keys. I quickly wish them goodnight as I reach into my purse to grab my cellphone and turn it on, and then I head out to the parking lot.

The drive back to the hotel flies by as I sing along with the radio. I'm just walking into my room, setting down my purse, thinking that I should probably start to pack up before grabbing some food since I have to drive back home first thing in the morning, when my phone starts ringing, Joshua's number popping up on the screen. I answer it, grinning as I bring the phone to my ear, impatiently waiting for the long recording to end so I can accept the call.

"How's my sexy little slut doing?"

The words echo over the line, catching me off guard and I frown. "Um, did you just call me a slut?"

Joshua chuckles. "I'm horny. Talk dirty to me."

I hesitate for three solid heartbeats, the blood draining from my face, and the high feeling I've been riding on since I left him fizzles away. I start stammering. Oh God, ten seconds on the phone and I've turned into a tongue-tied fool because this man wants me to talk sexy.

He laughs, amused. "Come on, baby. You can do this. I know you want to be my dirty little slut."

Sighing, I bury my face in my hand, saying nothing, not because I don't want to but because I can't. My throat is suddenly dry, my mouth glued shut, and for a second, I want to pretend I didn't answer the phone.

"Are you there?"

Crap. I wish I wasn't. I wish I wasn't sitting here, staring at the wall in my hotel room. I only just got back from the visit minutes before the phone rang. I should have stopped for food or gas or something ... anything.

"Yeah," I whisper. "I'm here."

"You looked so fucking sexy in those jeans today, baby," he rasps out. "And it turned me on so goddamn much hearing you say you love me."

I open my mouth to speak, and then stall as a recording plays, reminding us that the call is being recorded and monitored.

Shit.

Shit. Shit. Shit.

I'm getting so used to the recordings, hardly noticing them anymore, but at this minute all I can think about is some guard sitting there listening to us, listening to our private moment.

"I ... I don't know what to say," I whisper, my stomach

clenching. "I don't know … Can I just write you a story? I could do it tonight and mail it before I leave tomorrow."

As silly as it is, I want to be good at this for him.

I want him to be happy.

I want him to be happy with me.

And if I try this, there's a pretty high chance that I'm going to suck, but if I write him something …

"Did you pack some of your new toys like I asked?" he questions.

"Um, yeah," I say, nodding. "I did."

He hums into the phone, his voice dropping lower. "Why don't you go grab your vibrator and the vibrating plug for your ass?"

I purse my lips and narrow my eyes. I know what he's trying to do: make me relax by distracting me with an anal toy I haven't found the guts to try yet, but there's no cure for the nerves spinning in my stomach. Reluctantly, I say, "Okay."

Sighing, because I don't know how I'm going to do this, I stand up, crossing the room to my suitcase. I take my time digging (stalling) for the toys, almost wishing I'd never packed them.

Almost.

I'd considered it, stressing over what the border patrol might think if they searched my bags and found a bunch of vibrators. *Embarrassing.* But Joshua asked me to pack them, and the truth is, our phone sex thrills me. Thrills me in ways I've never been thrilled before even if I haven't had the guts to do much more than moan my way through it yet.

I just couldn't *not* pack them.

"Okay," I say, pulling the toy bag out of my suitcase and opening it up. I take out the toys he asked for along with the lube, and then toss the toy bag back into my suitcase. "I've got them."

"I want you to get naked, then lay back in the bed and turn on the vibrator," he instructs. "Rub it on your clit and relax. Get that pussy all nice and wet, but don't push it inside you until I tell you, okay?"

I swallow hard, placing the toys and lube on the nightstand, and then doing as he says, stripping off my clothing, before crawling under the covers, turning on the vibrator. "Okay."

"Good girl," he says, and hums. "Now picture this. I'm sitting in bed, watching some TV when you come in. You're wearing those sexy-ass yoga pants you like so much, and a skin-tight tank top. You walk by me to the closet, and I nearly groan at the sight of your thick, round ass, jiggling as you walk by."

I let out a giggle, though it sounds like more of a muffled moan. "I don't think I'll ever get used to you loving my big butt."

"You better," he says. "That ass of yours is sexy as fuck."

He pauses for a beat, listening to my breathing, as I rub my clit. "I come up behind you, turning you around, and I grip your ass, pulling you close until our lips meet. It's like fireworks going off as my tongue darts into your mouth. I can feel you pressing your crotch against me and my dick starts hardening."

Fireworks indeed.

I can feel them, the tiny sparks along my skin.

My pussy is wet—soaking wet—and aching, and I find myself relaxing, all my nerves fizzling away as I enjoy the sound of his voice.

"I pull away and start kissing your neck," he says, his voice dropping low to a whisper. "I want to fuck you while you have a vibrator in that tight little asshole of yours."

My breath comes quicker, my body heating up and all the emotions trapped within my chest, fear, excitement, anxiety, come out on a groan.

Joshua continues, his voice deep and raspy, "Tugging off your shirt, and pushing down your pants and panties, I kiss my way down to your breast and start sucking on your nipple, getting it nice and hard before moving to your other one, giving it the same attention, and then I tell you to lay down on the bed, and you do. I grab the toy and I show it to you, telling you to relax as my hands trail up your thighs."

"Joshua," I groan. "I need the vibrator inside me. Please."

I'm breathless.

I'm breathless and hurting in a delicious kind of way.

"Not yet," he says. "I want you to grab the vibrating plug and lube, and get it ready, baby."

I hesitate. The thought of it, of using anal toys turns me on, but actually doing it ... well, I don't know. "Is it going to hurt?"

"Probably," he says. "But I promise you, you'll like it in the end."

"O ... okay." I'm shaky, and edgy, as I do what he says, squirting some lube on the plug, getting it ready. When it is, I whisper, "I'm ready, I think."

Silence falls.

It's a breathless silence, full of anticipation and excitement.

I place the plug at my tight little bud, putting some pressure on it, trying to work it in, and then I freeze. Pain, not intolerable, but definitely uncomfortable, holds me still.

"It—" I let out a sharp breath. "Hurts."

"Just relax, love," he murmurs. "Work it in and out. Relax."

I try. I really, really try to relax, but it's an impossible task. The pain is sharp and it's so hard to keep a steady pressure, as I work it in and out. I make a sound, a groan or a moan, I'm not quite sure, and then, biting my bottom lips—hard—I push the plug all the way in.

"Did you glide it in, baby?" he murmurs.

I lick my lips nervously, and breathlessly, I respond, "Yes."

"How does it feel?"

"I don't know," I say, my voice shaky. "It hurts, but it also feels ... different. Good almost."

"Good, baby," he murmurs soothingly. "Now turn it on, then I want you to push the vibrator into your pussy and tell me how it feels while you're doing it."

Pressing the button on the plug, it buzzes to life, making me moan. My body starts to buck as I add the vibrator to the mix, making me pant. I'm so wet that it doesn't take a whole lot of effort to slide it in.

Jesus, it shouldn't feel this good, this intense.

"It feels ... good," I say, spreading my legs wider apart, moaning again. "I feel full. So ... good."

"Good, baby," he says, his voice changing, sounding rougher than before, raspy. "I can feel the pre-come dripping down my hard length. Your legs are wide open, and I slowly press my cock inside your pussy, pushing it all the way in. Your legs wrap around me and I lean down and start kissing you. Your breasts are pressed against my pecs and I can feel your heart beating out of your chest."

My eyes roll back from the pleasure and I cry out. It's just so ... intense, so different. I feel like I'm soaring higher and higher, so high I'm not sure I'll ever hit the ground again.

"As one hand grips your ass, I pull my cock out, and push it back in. I can feel the vibrations of the plug that's deep inside your asshole, buzzing against my cock as I'm pushing in and out of your tight little pussy. It feels so fucking good. I love feeling you stretched out to the max. I love sliding my cock in and out of you."

I moan—loud—my breath coming faster and faster. I don't even know what to do with the feelings inside me or how to describe them.

It's good.

It's amazing.

It's ... another moan pours out of me.

"That's right, baby, let go for me, Victoria," he murmurs. "I start kissing you and your nails dig into my back. I can feel your pussy clenching down around me. Every time I pull my cock out, you use your thighs, pulling me back in. I push up a little bit, staring into your eyes as I work my cock in and out, letting you know that I don't want to be anywhere else but here. My hand glides up and I grip your throat. You moan a little bit louder, and I stare into your eyes as my hand tightens, choking you, holding you still. Fuck, I love looking into those gorgeous green eyes, knowing you couldn't go anywhere unless I let you."

I moan at the mental image, oddly feeling even more aroused. I can almost feel his hand on my throat, and if the reality is anything like the image conjuring in my mind, I wouldn't mind it.

Not even a little.

I'd give up total control to this man in a heartbeat.

My body clenches tight, heat unraveling in my belly, as I start to thrash. "I'm going to come," I moan softly. "It feels so good … I can't …" Another moan slips out, my body tightening. "I'm … I'm … I'm coming."

Pure, hot ecstasy spreads through my body, my body clenching and clasping on the two toys within me, the vibrations shooting sparks through me. I gasp from the sensations, arching and twisting beneath the sheets, shuddering through an explosive orgasm.

He hums, the sound vibrating through the line. "Tell me my little slut is coming."

I don't hesitate. "Your little slut's coming."

"Again," he demands.

"Your little slut's coming." My voice is ragged and breathless.

"You're so fucking sexy, you know that, right?"

"Really?" I rasp out, feeling dazed and relaxed as I turn off the toys. So very, very relaxed.

"Really," he says. "Do you feel good, baby girl?"

"Yeah. Really good."

"Good." Oh God, I can hear the smile in his voice. "Now talk dirty to me."

I stir from my dazed, relaxed state, swallowing down a swell of anxiety, and nod my head against the pillow. "Okay."

That's it.

That's all I say.

My mind just … blanks. I can't think, can't picture anything. It's all just … blank. A dark void of nothingness.

I laugh. It's awkward and nervous and loud, and oh my God, did I just snort a little?

Crap, I did.

"Relax, baby girl. It's just you and me."

"Okay," I say, clearing my throat, although when I continue my voice is still a barely audible whisper. "Okay, I like giving blow jobs so can I try talking about that?"

He hums. "Talk about anything you want, baby."

"Okay," I say, nodding again. "Picture me, uh, on my knees in front of you. I lick my lips, reaching for your ..."

The one-minute left recording sounds, cutting me off, and I smile, relief almost crippling me. I let out a breath. I have no idea where I was going with that.

"You did good, baby," he says, and he sounds like he means it. "I'm really proud of you for trying that new toy."

"Thank you," I say. "I'm glad I tried it."

"I'm going to go jerk off," he says. "I'll call you later. Love you."

He hangs up then, and I flop back on the bed, staring up at the ceiling, thinking that I seriously need to call up one of those phone sex lines and get some pointers.

14

That's It, I'm Done

──────────

"You're home."

My footsteps falter in the middle of the foyer, the door just barely clicking shut behind me. I hesitate, glancing up at Richard standing at the bottom of the stairs, wearing only a pair of jeans. The button is hanging open, and the fly, only zipped halfway, as though he was rushing, tugging them on when he heard the door open. He looks surprised to see me, surprised and a little happy, too. It's odd ... "I am."

I take off my coat, hanging it in the closet, before kicking off my shoes and putting them away. When I turn back around, he's still standing there, cold eyes boring into me.

I hesitate, eyeing him back, before saying, "I'm going to go grab a shower, then go to bed."

──────────

The corner of his lip twitches, but it's not with amusement. He walks a few steps in my direction, and then pauses, his jaw clenching and unclenching, his eyes flaring. "I wouldn't recommend that. Come sit down for a minute. There's something we need to discuss."

My shoulders sag and I close my eyes for a beat. It's a little after eleven o'clock at night, and I've been driving all day. God, I'm too tired to deal with his shit today. Too exhausted from the drive to even think.

With a long sigh, I follow him into the living room, walking over to the couch and sitting down. "What's going on?"

He doesn't answer my question, instead, asking one of his own as he sits down on the loveseat across from me. "Did you have fun?"

I hesitate to respond; the coldness I feel from him putting me on edge. "Yes, I did. The drive was kind of boring and long, but overall it was a fun trip."

"Huh," he says, eyeing me curiously. He leans back, folding his arms over his bare chest. "Do you think you'll go again?"

My brows furrow at his question, but I nod. "Yup. I'm probably going to go back in a couple months."

"Huh," he says again. He doesn't look the least bit impressed by my answer.

Whatever.

There's a breath of silence, and then, "I have company."

I blink at him, shocked. I shouldn't be surprised, he's

hosted business guests here numerous times, but I am. I'm stunned he didn't let me know. Floored, actually. "Okay."

He nods. "You weren't supposed to be back until tomorrow."

I roll my eyes. "I sent you a message, one that you read. You knew I'd be back tonight."

"Huh," he says, his lips twitching again, but this time I see the amusement hidden behind the annoyance. "I must have forgotten."

I know there's a point to this conversation. He's gearing up for something, he always is, but at this moment, I don't care.

I'm too tired to care.

"Richard," I say, a hint of annoyance leaking into my voice. "I'm tired and I need a shower. We can do whatever this is tomorrow."

I move to stand up, but his voice stops me. "You should probably do all of that somewhere else tonight."

"What?" I ask, cutting my eyes to him.

"Like I said, I have company," Richard says. "I suppose you could use one of the guest bedrooms, although I'd prefer it if you just … vanished until I leave tomorrow." A wide grin splits his face. "I wouldn't want Julia to feel uncomfortable."

I stare at him.

And stare.

He wouldn't want Julia to feel uncomfortable?

And I stare some more.

Who's Julia?

And then ... I clue in.

He has company.

It's not a client or coworker.

He has a woman over.

In my house.

In my bed.

Instead of putting me on guard, the idea intrigues me. Is he finally moving on? My eyes widen. "You have a woman over? You brought her here? To our house?"

"Of course I did," he says, sounding proud of himself. "Any man in my situation would."

I laugh once. "And what exactly is your situation?"

"My wife is a lying, cheating whore," he says, matter-of-factly. "But I figure, now we're even."

We're even? I stare at him. I don't know what to say. I'm flabbergasted. I'm annoyed. I'm tired. I'm ... relieved? Yes, beneath the slow burn of irritation, there's relief.

I shrug noncommittally.

I don't let my spiking anger show, don't want to give him the satisfaction of seeing the outrage simmering through me. He might take it the wrong way. Might think that I give a shit about his little affair, rather than simply annoyed that I'm not in bed, or better yet, not still in Pennsylvania with Joshua.

I can't believe I came home for this.

"Jesus, you're an asshole." I exhale loudly. "I've never lied to you. I've never cheated on you. We've been over for months. How the fuck can you say I'm a cheating whore when you're the one with another woman in our bed?"

His eyes drift over me, and he's quiet for a moment. I wait for him to say more, watching as a nasty smile lifts his lips.

"Is that right?" He sounds genuinely interested. "We're over? I was under the impression that we were trying to work things out."

My skin starts to heat; my knees bounce. I continue breathing, though it feels like a challenge. He keeps looking at me, his eyes straight on my face, watching for something, waiting perhaps for me to freak-out.

I feel like freaking-out.

He has *Julia* upstairs in our bed and he still thinks we're trying to work things out?

Right, there's a woman in my bed.

A woman that's not me.

Jesus, I'm tired.

Maybe I should go up there, kick her out, and throw a fit, but it seems like a hell of a lot of work.

"You're delusional," I say, laughing. "You know damn well there's nothing left here, nothing for us to work out. I don't love you. I haven't loved you for a while now and you know it."

"And yet," he says, laughing under his breath, "you're still here. Living in my house."

"It's not your house," I say through clenched teeth as my

face flushes, frustration heating my cheeks. "I own just as much of it as you do."

"Choose your words carefully, pumpkin," he says quietly, his gaze hardening on mine. "Or you might not like what I do next."

"Oh, yeah?" I snap, my voice turning harsh and just as cold as his. "And what exactly are you going to do?"

Slowly, he leans forward, his eyes fixed on mine as he places his elbows on his knees. "I wonder what the world would think of a married romance writer carrying on a relationship behind her husband's back with a convicted murderer. I'm curious. Do you think if your readers knew what you're up to, they'd still buy your books?"

He says it without an ounce of hesitation, and I stare at him, stunned. "You wouldn't."

"Trust me, sweetheart, I would," he says. "If you don't stop talking to that asshole, I'll ruin you. I'll take everything, *every-fucking-thing.* You'll have no one to help you, nowhere to go. When I'm done, the only thing you'll have left is that piece of shit killer."

Something happens to me then, something that I can't even explain. A calm settles over me, but at the same time rage crashes through me. Flashes of the last three years flood my mind. Tears and heartache and anger fill the majority of them.

God, were we ever happy together?

If we were, I can't see it ... can't feel it.

"That's it," I say, my voice a breathless whisper. "I'm done."

And I mean it this time.

I'm well and truly done.

He flinches when I say it, his expression falling as his gaze settles on me, his cold eyes staring me down. He laughs once. "I can't believe I wasted three years of my life on you. I swear to God you and your little convict are going to pay for the bullshit you've put me through these last few months."

Those words make me tremble. His tone isn't sharp, but it's definitely serious. It's not an empty threat, I don't think. My skin tingles, that frosty look in his eyes freezing my blood. I believe him, believe that he won't rest until he's destroyed my life, but knowing that doesn't change my mind. Maybe I should stay with him, but I don't want to.

I don't think I can.

"What do you want from me?"

He says nothing as he stares at me. Nothing about what he wants from me, but somehow, I already know.

He wants me.

It sends a chill down my spine.

"Richard, please," I say, hating the desperation I hear in my voice. "I can't do this anymore. It's over. It's been over for a long time."

"Maybe." He shrugs. "If you want to leave, then leave.

I'm not stopping you, but you screwed me, and I promise you, if you leave I'll screw you just as hard."

"Who are you?" I ask. "Where's that nice man I married? You weren't always this ... bitter, this ... vindictive."

"I am the same—" He pauses for a beat, shaking his head. "I haven't changed, Vic. You're the one that's changed."

I can't really argue with that.

Guilty.

I have changed.

But so has he.

"The way I see it, you've got a choice here," he says after a moment. "You can cut him out of your life and stay. I'll forget all of this and we can move on. Or you can leave. I'll go to the media with your story, and your father. I'll make sure everyone knows what a whore you are. I'll destroy your business and your name, and then I'll take everything that's left. Every goddamn penny."

I swallow hard. "You couldn't. All of this is just as much mine as it is yours."

"Maybe you're right," he says coolly. "But are you willing to lose your career for a murderer?"

"Stop calling him that!"

"Why?" he asks. "That's what he is. A coldblooded murderer."

I can see what he's trying to do here, the doubt he's trying to plant. "I think I hate you."

He stares at me for a moment. "You should feel lucky. I'm willing to forget it all. All you have to do is cut him out of your life."

I laugh. Lucky? Nothing about this makes me feel lucky.

Richard stands up then, walking toward the stairs. He pauses at the bottom, glancing back at me. "I'm taking Julia to the Hawaii beach house for a couple weeks. Think about it, sweetheart. I expect your decision by the time I get back."

I sit there for a moment, hesitating, watching as Richard disappears upstairs, before finally getting up and walking back out the door, grabbing my bag as I leave.

There's nothing to think about.

Nothing at all.

I put my bag back in the trunk and get into my car, starting it up as I dig for my phone in my purse. Finding it, I shoot off a quick text to Becca.

ME: Are you home?

BECCA: Yup. What's up?

ME: Richard has a visitor of the woman variety. Mind if I crash with you tonight?

BECCA: WTF? He's cheating? R U OK?

ME: I'm fine. Great, actually. It's finally over.

BECCA: Yay! *Happy Dance* The door's open. C U soon.

ME: Thanks.

It's a fifteen-minute drive to Becca's house. I turn on the radio, blasting the music, and try to think of something—anything—except the reality of my situation.

By the time I make it there, I've almost convinced myself that Richard's threats were empty. He won't go to the media. He's too worried about his reputation to shine a spotlight on our failing relationship. I turn into Becca's driveway, parking behind her silver Focus, and slip the car in park, turning it off.

Becca had turned on the outside light for me. Getting out, I pull my bag out of the trunk and pad up to the house, letting myself in.

"Becca?" I call out as I close the door behind me, locking it as I dump my bag at the door.

"In the kitchen," she calls out.

Kicking off my shoes, I head down the entry hallway, and step into the large kitchen, stalling at the doorway when I spot Becca standing at the island, pouring two shots of tequila.

Shit.

Shit. Shit. Shit.

I don't want to talk. Not tonight. Maybe not ever.

"Shit, babe," Becca mutters, giving me a thorough onceover. "You look awful. Are you okay?"

Sighing, I walk over to the island and hop up onto one of the tall bar-style stools. "That's because I've been driving all day."

She lets out a dry laugh and slides a shot over to me. "Right. Drink up. It'll make you feel better."

I cut my eyes at her. "A shower and a good night's sleep will make me feel better."

"Okay, fine," she says, sitting down beside me and offering me a small smile. The sight of it makes me feel a little more at ease. "Drink up. It'll make *me* feel better."

I laugh, shaking my head. "Fine, but I don't want to talk about it. Not tonight."

"Sure ..." Becca grins, and then downs her shot. "So, is Joshua as hot in person as his pictures?"

I smile at her. God, I love my best friend. "He's even hotter."

15

Google Is Not My Friend

———————

Richard didn't get to me.

He didn't.

Not even a little.

Joshua isn't a coldblooded murderer.

I click on another Google headline, this one reading: Who Brings Guns To A Bar Brawl?

Joshua Larson, age twenty-one, has been sentenced to eight years in prison, with an extra four years of extended supervision, after shooting a man during a bar brawl.

I scan through the article, and then use the find function, searching for one word: knife. Nothing. None of the articles mention finding the knife that the other man supposedly had. On the contrary, they all say it was never found.

Returning to my search, I click on another heading: Joshua Larson Receives Maximum Sentence.

And then I click on another: Joshua Larson Beats 1st Degree Murder Charge, But Convicted On Another.

Larson claimed self-defense, although this wasn't particularly believable. He went to the bar that night wearing his motorcycle gang colors and armed with a .38. This was not a man intending to drink in peace.

God, they're all the same. The articles all reference his membership in a motorcycle club and the fact that he was wearing his colors. They talk about the victim, though none gives a clear picture of what the fight was even about.

Leaning back in my chair, I click the back button, returning to my search. God, I wish Becca didn't have to work today. Her house is too ... quiet without her here. Nearly as lonely as mine.

It's a little before ten o'clock in the morning and I'm already tired, exhausted really, and kind of hungry.

I need food.

And a nap.

I should probably go home. I bet Richard is already on a plane by now; he always books morning flights, but sleeping in that house, in the bed that he just shared with another woman, doesn't sound appealing. Not even a little.

Is it crazy that I'm still missing Joshua even while reading these articles?

Probably.

I'm a goddamn mess.

He's called twice already this morning, and I've ignored them both, but damn it, I feel lonely as hell, missing a man who I'm beginning to think I have no business missing.

"Oh, Google, I thought we were friends," I mutter to the computer as I scroll through yet another article. "You're not being a very good friend right now."

My phone rings for the third time. I glance at it, seeing Joshua's number flashing across the screen once again. Growing frustrated with my searches and the ringing, I finally answer it, accepting the call.

"My beautiful angel, what are you up to?"

The sound of his voice makes me smile. God, I love the way the sound causes my belly to dip a little.

"Not much," I say, not wanting to admit that I've been googling him for the last few hours. "Sorry I missed your calls this morning."

"It's okay," he says. "I figured you'd probably sleep in today after that drive."

I wish I had slept in.

Silence falls. I don't respond, because admitting that I was simply ignoring his calls doesn't sound like a good plan.

"So talk to me, baby girl. Why are you so quiet this morning?"

"Well, Richard's having an affair," I say right away. "She was at the house when I got home last night, and he's taking her to our house in Hawaii for a couple weeks."

"Baby girl," he says, his voice turning concerned. "I'm sorry you had to see that."

He means it. I can hear the sincerity in his voice. But his soothing tone punctures a hole in me and like a flash flood, all my stress and anxiety and fear comes pouring out.

"He's going to ruin my life if I don't stay with him," I cry. My eyes are burning, tears welling up and leaking out no matter how quickly I try to blink them away. "He's going to ruin my name and my books and ... and ..." A sob chokes me and I gasp in a ragged breath. "He's going to ..."

"Baby," he says gently, cutting me short. "You need to pull it together, okay? Everything's going to be okay. We'll figure all this out."

How? How is it going to be okay? I want to scream the question, but I don't. I can't.

"Okay," I whisper instead, nodding my head and sniffling. "Okay."

He's quiet for a beat, taking a deep breath. "Are you upset he's cheating?"

"No." My response is immediate, and perhaps a little too quick to make it believable, but it's true. I'm not upset about that. I'm ... glad. Happy, even. I'm definitely relieved that it's finally over.

"You sure?" he asks.

"I'm sure," I tell him softly.

"Alright," he says, though his tone tells me he's still not one-hundred percent sure I'm telling the truth. He pauses for a second, before stating, "I've got to tell you, I'm not really surprised he's pulling this shit. I knew something was going to happen while you were away and with me."

His statement causes my spine to snap straight and the last of my tears dry up. I frown. "How could you possibly know that?"

I didn't know. Maybe I'm a fool, but when Richard said I should go and meet Joshua, even if his delivery was malicious and hurtful, I believed he was okay with it. I thought he really wanted me to figure things out.

"Once someone does something once," he says, "they're willing to do it again, and Richard has been threatening you in one way or another since you married him."

Once someone does something once …

No, stop. Don't even think about that. This isn't about Joshua. It isn't.

Oh, who am I kidding?

This is all about Joshua.

I rub my hands roughly across my face. "He told me I have to choose, you or him. And if I don't stay with him, he's going to go to the media with my story and ruin my career."

I wait for Joshua's response. He sighs long and loud. "Well, beautiful, if he does that, would that really even hurt your career? You're a romance author that fell in love. Your readers will love it."

Dammit! Why is he so calm about this?

I shut my eyes, trying to relax my stiff muscles, and take a couple deep breaths. Okay. Maybe he's on to something here. Would my readers care about this? Is it possible they'd think that a relationship with a convict is romantic? Sexy even?

Possibly.

But my dad ...

"He threatened to tell my dad everything so he knows what a little slut I am."

"Well, I really hope he wouldn't stoop that low," he says, and I can hear the scowl in his voice. "Maybe he's just angry and it's an empty threat, but would your family really care what he has to say? Your dad raised you, he knows who you are and what you're like. I don't think he'd even listen to Richard."

"I don't know. I haven't told him about you." I laugh once. "I can't see my dad approving of me writing to someone in prison, let alone me dating someone in prison."

"I completely understand that," he says, his voice genuine and not the least bit surprised. "I wouldn't want my sisters talking to someone in prison nor dating them. But we found love and one of these days, you're going to have to tell your family, and when you feel like you're ready to tell them, that's the time to do it. There's no rush for anything."

I shut my eyes once again. How can he be so calm about this? I don't know, but he sure levels me out. Five minutes on the phone and all of this doesn't seem that bad.

How the hell does he do it? How does he change me from a sobbing, frazzled ball of nerves to feeling ... peaceful?

We're different, so, so different. Our lives, our personalities. He's used to violence, confronting his issues head on, where I'm more of the stress quietly type.

And yet, here we are. I'm obsessed with him, and I have a feeling he isn't too far behind me.

He's special, I think, and I swear, he was made just for me.

"I wasn't sleeping in this morning," I confess. "I ignored your calls because I was Googling you again."

"Why?"

"Because," I say shamefully, "Richard got to me last night and well, what if I'm making a mistake with you? What if this is all a huge mistake?"

"What if it's not?" he prods. "What if you don't give us your all and this is your one chance to be happy for the rest of your life. You know if you don't try this with me, if you just stop now, that for the rest of your life you'll be thinking about the 'what ifs.'"

He's right. I know it, feel it, but still ...

"They don't say very nice things about you online. They

say you were out looking for a fight, that you aren't a good man."

"Beautiful," he says on a deep exhale, "I've told you before, I don't like you Googling me. Half the things they wrote online are lies. All the media want people to do is read it. It's not even accurate. You know the real me, baby."

"Do I?" I ask, my voice dropping as regret tightens my chest. I stare at the computer blankly, suddenly wishing I'd never turned it on.

We had such great visits.

We were happy.

I was happy.

"Baby, you—" He stalls, letting out a sigh. "Of course you do. What you saw over the weekend is exactly who I really am. This isn't a game to me. I truly love you and I want to spend the rest of my life with you."

Silence falls.

It's long. It's awkward. I try to break it, but my mouth isn't working, my voice stuck in my throat.

And then, the one-minute warning sounds.

"I'll call you right back, okay?"

He doesn't wait for my response before hanging up. I toss my phone down, waiting for it to ring again.

It does.

Reaching for it, I pick it up and answer the call. I swear the recording takes forever this time, far longer than it ever has before. When I'm finally prompted to accept the call, I do, and then I wait for it to connect.

"I don't trust you sitting there, living with Richard," Joshua says right away. "You need to just leave him. Slowly, he's been getting worse and worse and I'm afraid one day he might do something that you won't be able to come back from."

I scoff. "He won't do anything."

And I'm ninety-nine percent sure of that. Richard is not the violent type. He yells, he says hurtful things, but he wouldn't physically hurt me.

It's just not his style.

"You say that now, baby, but you probably didn't think he'd threaten to ruin your career if you leave him. Or that he'd call your father and tell him what a whore he thinks you are. So I really don't think you know him too well, because if you did, you would have seen this coming."

My stomach knots. "What if I don't know you as well as I think I do? Everything I saw online ... it just ... you're not the sweet guy you show me."

"Every time you read something online, it's going to make you question me," he says, "but deep down in your heart you know that the guy you see is who I am."

I laugh sharply, my stomach twisting tighter. "I thought I really knew who Richard was, too."

"But baby, you were never in love with Richard the way you're in love with me now."

"Yeah, you're right," I say, an angry bite to the words. "So now I'm blinded by love. How can I even trust what I think or feel with you?"

My response makes him chuckle, genuinely amused. "Is that so bad to be in love? People try their whole lives to find what we've found together. And yeah, I'm in prison, but one day I won't be and if we can make it through this, the hardest part of our relationship, the rest of our lives will be easy. These couple years will seem like nothing when we're ninety years old, lying in bed together."

I laugh once, twice, three times, and then it just pours out of me, nerves, I think, and it takes a moment for me to stop. "I don't even want to think about being ninety years old."

"As long as I'm next to you," he says, "it doesn't matter, baby."

His tone is gentle, and it sends all the longing in me rocketing to my heart. I exhale through my nose, trying to keep my heart from bursting, and ask the question that's been plaguing me from the start. "Was it really self-defense?"

"You know the answer to that, my love," he says calmly. "Of course it was. I had no choice."

"I'm really scared," I say quietly, feeling inadequate. He's all man, and I'm probably no more than a helpless, terrified woman to him. "I hate being this scared. I don't know what to do."

"I'm scared, too, baby," he admits, his voice barely a whisper. "But we're a team. If we stick together and stand by each other, we'll get through this. That's all that matters."

He's scared? I swallow hard, clutching my phone tighter. I can't imagine Joshua Larson being scared of anything, but I hope like hell he means that, because dammit if his admittance doesn't make the butterflies wake up in my belly.

I hesitate. "What am I going to do about Richard?"

"I'm pretty sure the threats are just a scare tactic so you'll stop talking to me and stay with him," he says. "But you know you don't belong with him. You're extremely unhappy there. He makes you extremely unhappy. I think you should get a lawyer and get ahead of this thing."

A lawyer, right.

"Right, okay," I say calmly, squaring my shoulders and taking a deep breath. "I need to find a lawyer."

"And," he says. "I'd like it if you moved closer to me."

I blink, surprised. "Really?"

Joshua chuckles. "Really. You belong to me and you know this. I want you closer."

Holy shit. Did he just say that?

I know I've said it before, that he's asked me to say it, but it was just a sex thing.

I *thought* it was just a sex thing.

My heart races. "Did you just say I belong to you?"

"Yeah, baby, I did and you know you do," he says, and I can hear the smile in his voice. "Deep down in your heart you know you belong to me, that you're meant to be with just me."

Yes! I want to scream it, yell it from the rooftops, but

somehow I manage to hold it back, instead responding coyly, "Maybe."

"Just maybe?" He hums. "I don't even think you believe it, baby. You know you do, so why fight it?"

And then, once again, that damn one-minute warning plays on the line.

"Baby, it's almost count time," he says. "I'll give you a call back as soon as I can. Just know that all I want is a life with you. I want to make you happy. I want to make you smile, feel beautiful and loved every single day of your life. I love you."

The phone disconnects then, and as I set it down, I realize I'm smiling.

He loves me and I really do belong to him.

16

Family Law Sucks

"I understand what you're saying, Mrs. Clarke, but he's still entitled to a share of your business."

I blink at the lawyer, then blink again. "But he makes so much more than me."

"I understand," she says, "but the courts will look at your potential earnings when making a decision, which, according to the market, is far higher than his. Since you began your publishing company after you married him, a judge would most likely award him a fifty-percent ownership of your company."

Wait. What?

I squirm in my seat. This can't be happening. After all this, all the bullshit he's put me through, he can't be allowed to win. "But I don't want anything from him. I don't need his money. Doesn't that change anything?"

She shuffles some papers around, making a neat little pile, her eyes narrowed in contemplation. "That's a good question," she says eventually. "Since Nova Scotia family law is 50/50, legally, upon divorce, you're required to equalize your assets. Basically, each party should leave the marriage on equal grounds. So he can still sue for his half of the marital assets, and your publishing company is an asset. He may never see a penny, though. It all depends on your earnings. For him to collect, you would have to out-earn him."

Right. Of course he can.

I laugh once. "You've got to be kidding me."

"Your best bet, if he's amicable, is to settle this outside of court. Drafting a separation agreement is top priority. I don't advise it, but if you're certain you want nothing out of this marriage, we'll aim for having a no support and no property division clause, and with luck, he'll agree to that. If not, I'd strongly advise reevaluating your stance on this matter."

"Family law sucks," I mutter, leaning back in my chair, my lungs deflating in a quick burst of air as though she just punched me in the gut.

No. Scratch that.

A quick hit would probably be easier to handle than this.

My comment makes her laugh. "Marriage in Nova

Scotia is looked at as a partnership. It's business, Mrs. Clarke. We're a no fault, 50/50 province. In some cases, this could *suck*, but it can also be beneficial."

I nod. I can see that. Maybe where there's a stay-at-home mom, but for my situation, well, it just sucks.

I sigh heavily. "What about his threats?"

She straightens in her chair, folding her hands on the table in front of her. "Until he acts on them, there's nothing we can do. If he does go to the media with your story, there may be some legal recourse for you."

"But there's no way to stop him, no guarantee a judge would rule in my favor if he tries to ruin my name."

She shakes her head. "If his allegations are true, and he can prove that, then no, there's no guarantee. The only promise I can make to you is that if you retain me, I will do everything I can to protect your assets and your business."

I nod. I don't know what to say, what to do. The man could very well ruin my life and there's nothing, *nothing*, I can do about it.

"My initial retainer is seven-thousand," she continues. "I'm confident that we can settle this matter with that."

Seven-thousand. I squirm in my chair as her price sinks in. It seems like such a waste of money, really, though I'd pay that to see the look on Richard's face when he realizes how costly this divorce will be if he chooses to fight me.

Shit. I'd pay double her retainer just to see that.

That's when it hits me. A thought—a longshot—but a thought nonetheless forms, and a genuine smile forms on my lips. "Thank you, Ms. Lane," I say, gathering up all my financials and paperwork. "I'd like to go ahead with the agreement as discussed. Let's see if he'll go for a clean and simple separation."

She stands up, shaking my hand, and has me pay the retainer through her secretary, assuring me that she'll draft something up for my review right away, and then I'm on my way, back into the chilly October air.

Pulling my jacket closed, I head to the parking lot, glancing at my phone. It's just before eleven o'clock in the morning; Joshua will be calling soon.

Getting into my car, I start it up and turn the heat up full blast, before I whip the car out of the parking lot.

It's a twenty-minute drive to my house from the lawyer's office. I stop at a U-Haul store and purchase a crap-ton of boxes, then at a Starbucks, ordering a Caramel Macchiato, and sip on it as I wait for my phone to ring, trying to think of something—anything—but the meeting I just had or the packing I have to do.

By the time I'm halfway home, I'm feeling okay, having a little more clarity on how I need to approach my divorce, and when my phone finally rings, I answer it, putting it on speakerphone, and accept the call.

"Hey. What's good, baby girl?"

"Everything's good," I say, clipping the phone into the holder on the dash. "I just got out of the lawyer's office and now I'm heading home to start packing."

"Good." He sounds pleased, like maybe he thought I

wouldn't actually go to my appointment. Or perhaps it's that he thought I'd chicken out and not move out of the house. "How did it go, my love?"

"I don't really know," I say. "It was kind of confusing. She said he could go after my business because of my earning potential."

"Is that something you think he'd do?" he asks.

I laugh once. *Probably.* "I don't even know. Honestly, I don't know what to think about any of it. She doesn't seem to agree with me on what I want to do, but she did agree to give it a try, though she said if he doesn't agree to my terms, then I need to reevaluate everything."

"Well, do you feel comfortable with her? Like, do you think she's a good lawyer and will be on your side?"

"Yeah, I like her," I say. "I just think, maybe she'll try to push me to fight for something."

He lets out a deep sigh. "Baby girl, I really don't think you should walk away with nothing. You shouldn't be getting screwed because he's an asshole."

Fair enough, but I'm pretty sure fighting him in court will screw me.

"Yeah, but what if we can convince him to sign off on leaving me and my business alone?" I ask. "I don't need his money, Joshua. I make more than enough on my own."

And he will sign off. Once he wraps his head around how much he'll have to give me, he'll be willing to settle quietly.

I'm sure of it.

I hope.

"Baby, just because you're offering to walk away from everything doesn't mean he'll go for it," he says. "I really think that you need to just do what's in your best interest. And with the way he's been behaving lately, I don't really trust him."

"I still think that maybe I should try to do it this way. I won't touch any of his stuff, and in return he won't touch mine. I just want to get this done and over with. And I don't want anything from him. I don't want the reminders."

Silence falls and seconds pass.

Five, ten, fifteen seconds ... I count the seconds in my head, waiting for his thoughts, trying to think of a better way to make him see that trying to get Richard to settle quietly and privately isn't a bad thing.

"If that's what you think is best," he says, though the tone of his voice tells me something entirely different. "It's your company, your business, I would just hate to see you lose out because you don't want to fight for what you deserve."

I inhale deeply. "But I am fighting for what I deserve. I'm fighting for me. I'm fighting to get my life back. And I'm fighting for us. If I leave everything, then maybe, *maybe,* he won't ruin my life."

"Baby, he's just threatening you to try to control you," he says, a hint of anger in his voice. "That's all that is. We both know that. And he sees it's not working so he's just basically trying anything he can to get you to stay, no matter what, whether it's a threat toward your family, a threat toward me, it doesn't really matter. He's trying everything he can to get you to stay."

But why? I want to scream the question. The man doesn't love me. He can hardly tolerate me on most days. Why the hell does he want me to stay? I just don't get it.

It makes no sense.

Not even a little.

"I just think I can use all of that to my advantage now," I say, swallowing down the well of anxiety creeping up my throat. "I just want to try at least. My lawyer is going to draft up an agreement and see what he says. Maybe he'll sign it and we can be done with this."

Joshua lets out a long sigh. "If you really feel like you can get him to sign off on not touching your business and everything like that, then that would be great, baby. I mean, it's worth it to try. I just think he's all over the place right now, and I just ... I don't really know what to think. He's done so many horrible things to you already."

"Well, at least he's not at home for a couple weeks," I say. "And by the time he gets back, I'll be gone. What's the worst he can do? Call me and yell at me? I can hang up on him."

"Okay, baby, well whatever you think is best."

He doesn't sound reassured, but he doesn't press this issue, and after a few minutes of random chitchat, he lets me go.

When I get home, I'm keyed-up, ready to get to work. I briefly consider calling my parents, but the thought doesn't last. I know they won't agree with me just walking away and leaving everything behind. And I don't think I can handle their reactions to my failing marriage or my relationship with Joshua. Not now.

I head straight for my office, carrying as many boxes as I can handle, piling them on the floor. Then, I fire off a quick text to Becca.

ME: I'm at my house, packing. Are you certain you don't mind me staying with you and using your garage as storage?

Her response comes quickly.

BECCA: Of course not. I'll be over once I'm finished at work to help. Love you, babe.

ME: Love you, too.

Setting my phone down, I pick up one of the boxes, and quickly put it together, before turning to my bookshelves. I try not to think as I take the first books off the beautiful shelves and pack them into the cardboard box, though it's a useless effort. With each book I place into the box, I think.

I think about this room, *my sanctuary.*

I think about this house.

I think about the good times and the bad times and everything in between.

I think.

And I remember.

And I hardly get anything done.

And when Becca walks in hours later, I'm still in my office working on clearing off my bookshelves. She walks into my office, her eyes scanning the few boxes I managed to fill, and I can tell from her expression that she isn't surprised I haven't gotten more done.

She looks sorry—sorry and sad.

"It's harder than you thought it'd be, isn't it?" she asks, her eyes flickering toward my filing cabinet, where I abandoned a half-filled box.

This was something I hadn't given much thought to last night when I asked her if I could crash with her for a little while. In fact, it didn't really hit me until I was about to go to sleep and she told me she'd help me pack my things and move them into her garage for now.

I told her it wasn't necessary, that I could just leave everything in the house until I figured things out.

She told me it'd be crazy not to, considering how erratic Richard has been acting. And she pointed out that even though he said he'd be gone for two weeks, he could fly home at any time and when he finds me gone, who knows what would happen to my things.

"Yeah, it is."

She steps over to the filing cabinet and pulls one of the drawers open. "It'll get easier, babe. Promise."

"Yeah, I'm sure it will." I grab some more books, feeling relieved and slightly more focused now that she's here. "So, um, Joshua asked me to move to Pennsylvania."

"He wants you to move out there?" she asks. "Already?"

Becca looks like I just hauled off and slapped her. Her eyes are so wide they look as though they could pop out at any second. She just stares at me with shock, and I almost feel guilty, smiling back at her timidly. We've been best friends since grade school, and the thought of moving so far away from her isn't a happy one.

"Yeah."

"Are you ready for that?"

I shrug. "I really don't know."

I turn to Becca as she flops down on the chair, staring off out the window, looking lost. After a moment, her skeptical gaze turns to me. "Have you told your parents yet?"

"No," I say, shaking my head. "I haven't told them about anything."

"You probably should," she says after a moment. "They should hear the story from you before Richard decides to tell them."

She's right. I know she is, but ...

"What if they don't approve of Joshua?"

"You'll deal," she says firmly. "Just like you dealt when they didn't approve of Richard."

17

Parents Know Best

———

My cellphone pings. I roll over in bed, picking it up from my nightstand to take a look. It's a text message from Richard.

RICHARD: I hear you're trying to screw me. I'm surprised you're willing to risk your reputation.

And then it pings again ...

RICHARD: You wait until I leave the country to pull this shit?

And again ...

RICHARD: After everything I've done for you over the last two years. Ruthless.

And again ...

RICHARD: I hope whatever money you get from me gets burned when you move on to the next guy. Maybe your boyfriend convict can use some for his canteen.

I sit up in bed as tears—damn tears—burn my eyes. Oh, shit, he knows I went to a lawyer. He knows. How the hell does he know already?

When my phone chimes again, I want to throw it across the room.

But I don't.

Of course I don't.

Call it curiosity if you want, but the masochist in me looks at the new message.

RICHARD: Did you really think I wouldn't have someone watching you while I was gone? I know you were at Matheson and Associates yesterday. Really, Victoria? I'm gone a day and you're already getting a lawyer?

I know I shouldn't respond. Poking the bear never helps, but I'm sick of keeping my mouth shut. Tired of letting him walk all over me, so I type a response, and send it.

ME: If you're going to be like this, then you can just speak to my lawyer. Obviously you already know who that is. I'm being more than fair here and really, if you bothered to wait for the proposal, you'd see that. Besides, you're the one who threatened me, I'm just trying to protect myself here.

And then I wait.
And I wait.
And I wait some more.
I'm about to get out of bed, thinking a nice hot shower will calm my nerves, when Richard finally responds.

RICHARD: Listen. Can you please stop acting like you're the victim? I'm the victim. I'm sure your father will agree ...

My father ... Anger flares, causing my tears to stream from my eyes and drip down my cheeks. What's wrong with him?

I take a deep breath, trying to calm myself, before I respond once more.

ME: You're not a victim, Richard. If you'd just wait for the papers from my lawyer, you'd see I'm being more than reasonable.

His response comes quickly this time, my phone chiming seconds after I send the message.

RICHARD: Yeah, I'm sure you're being reasonable.

And then it pings again.

RICHARD: If you think you're going to screw me, I'll make sure you leave with nothing.

I stare at the message.
And stare.
And then I stare some more.
I want to tell him off. I want to call him names and scream, but I don't.
I can't.
I just don't have the energy for it.
Turning my phone to vibrate, I set it back down on the nightstand and climb out of bed, my legs wobbly. Geez, why am I letting that asshole get to me like this? I sniffle once and scrub at my face, wiping any trace of my tears

away, and then I head to the bathroom, closing the door behind me.

I shower and shave and stress, the goddamn messages making me edgy. Maybe I'm crazy, but I was hoping—praying—that for once, Richard might be reasonable. I stay under the hot spray until my fingers and toes wrinkle, and then I get out and slather on lotion, making every inch of my body smell like vanilla bean. As I head back into my bedroom, hair and body wrapped in towels, I hear my phone vibrating against the oak nightstand.

Hesitating, I eye it for a beat before curiosity gets the best of me once again and I walk to it, glancing at the call display.

Joshua.

I answer it hesitantly, practicing smiling as I wait to accept the call, though it feels forced, anger and heartache still pulsing through my system. When the call finally clicks through, his voice greets me immediately. "Hey, gorgeous. Is everything okay?"

"Hey. Yeah, everything's good."

"I've been calling for twenty minutes. Where were you?"

There's a hint of concern in his voice, and a touch of bitterness that makes my stomach twist. My eyes fall down to the towel wrapped around me. "Um, I was in the shower," I say. "Sorry about that. I turned my phone on vibrate and didn't hear it ringing."

"Why's your phone on vibrate?" he asks.

My stomach is in knots. I don't want to tell him about the messages, not even a little, but I know I have to. Sighing, I mutter quietly, "Well, Richard knows I saw a lawyer yesterday."

He's silent for a moment. "Oh, yeah. I thought he was in Hawaii. How'd he find out already?"

"He said he has someone watching me. He started texting me this morning and they were pretty nasty so I turned off my ringer."

"Oh, baby, don't let him get to you," he says. "Give him a bit of time and when he calms down, tell him to talk to your lawyer. There's no reason for you to respond. Just let him calm down, baby. Everything's going to be okay. I promise."

I hesitate and my head starts throbbing, a dull ache right between the eyes as my anger reawakens, flowing through my body. "I did respond," I confess. "I told him that I was being reasonable and he could speak to my lawyer, and he said I'm trying to screw him, that he's a victim and my father would agree. How the hell am I trying to screw him? He's the one that's threatening to ruin my business. I don't get it. What have I done to screw him?"

"Baby," he says, and then sighs. "I don't think you've done anything. You've been perfectly honest. You told him you were writing me, you told him you were visiting me. You never lied to him, you never cheated on him, and if you're worried about him contacting your parents, maybe you should just get it over with and tell them first."

His words strike me hard. I never really doubted it, never really thought I was doing anything wrong, but ... "Do you really believe that? Do you really believe I haven't done anything wrong?"

"Oh, baby girl, yes, I do believe it," he confirms, his tone gentle, but it's suddenly a hard pill to swallow.

"Even though I was still living with him when I met you?"

"Victoria, you're an amazing woman and you did nothing wrong," his says firmly. "It was over between you two when we started writing. We fell in love, so why wouldn't we want to be together? I love you and I want you in my life."

I close my eyes, flinching at his words. "We've only spent ten hours together, face to face."

"They were the best ten hours of my life."

****

Two hours later, I'm back at my house. It's too quiet and my head is too loud. There's so many things I need to do, but I'm at a standstill, waiting for Richard to calm down. Waiting for my lawyer to finish the agreement.

The ball's out of my court.

I hate that I don't have any power.

I should be packing, but I'm not. I lay back on my bed,

too stressed to do much more than just lie here. My bed smells like laundry detergent, the sheets freshly washed. Richard must have washed them after screwing his new toy here. His messages won't leave my mind, his threats mingling in, replaying over and over, like a bad song stuck on repeat.

Sighing, I try to push him from my head and pick up my phone, scrolling through the contacts. Joshua's right. I need to call my parents before *Dick* does.

I make it down to their number, my finger hesitating above it. I have no idea what I'm going to say or what I'm going to do, but I do know my parents, and news like this is best done publicly. Glancing at the time, I see that it's eleven-thirty in the morning. Lunch. I can take them out for lunch.

It takes less than thirty seconds to convince my mom to meet me for lunch. My dad takes a little over a minute, but he agrees, and forty minutes later, I'm sitting at a table at Avanti's sipping on some water waiting for them to arrive.

A bell over the door chimes when they step inside, Mom two steps ahead of Dad. I stand up, waving her over, and when she spots me, her face splits with a smile.

"Victoria!" My mother rushes over, nearly sprinting for me. She wraps her arms around me as Dad comes up behind her, shaking his head.

"Hey, Mom," I say, hugging her back before wiggling out of her arms and wrapping mine around Dad. "Hey, Dad."

"I hope you haven't been waiting long?" Dad asks,

hugging me back before he takes a seat. "Your mother was dawdling."

"No worries," I say, smiling. "I only just got here myself."

Dad nods, his bright blue eyes regarding me curiously. "So what's this all about?"

"Can't I just want to have lunch with my parents?" I ask.

"Yes," he says, a small smirk curving his lips. "But if it were just lunch, we'd be sitting at my table while your mother made club sandwiches, not at a restaurant."

"Oh, George, give her a break," Mom says, cutting me an apologetic smile. "Enjoy yourself, will you? It's not very often we get to spend time with our little girl."

The waitress appears, asking what we would like to drink, and we place our orders, the entire time I'm acutely aware of Dad's probing gaze.

My stomach clenches as my brain works, trying to find the right way to start the conversation, but I'm pretty sure there's no right way to tell your parents that you're leaving your asshole husband and have fallen in love with a convicted murderer.

Right, there's no good way to do this.

Just get it over with, Vic.

Oh God, I want to puke.

Picking up my menu, I hide behind it, my voice barely a whisper when I say, "There's something I need to tell you guys. I screwed up and I don't want any of your judgment, so just listen to me and let me get it all out before you say anything."

Dad laughs. "I haven't heard you say that since you were sixteen."

"This isn't funny, Dad," I say, cutting him a look. "I really screwed up, and I don't know how to handle it."

And then, I launch into my story. I tell them about Richard, about how he's treated me since we married and what it's done to me. I tell them about Joshua, filling them in on the letters and the phone calls and visits. And I tell them all about Richard's threats and his affair, explaining that he's taken her to the Hawaii house and that Becca and I have been packing up all my things, barely pausing when the waitress returns with our drinks.

"Victoria," Mom says, reaching for my hand as Dad shoos the waitress away, asking her to give us a moment. "Sweetie, are you okay? You're looking a little green."

I force a quick shake of my head. "No. No, I'm really not okay. Richard and I are splitting up and he's being an asshole about it."

Dad's smile disappears and he leans back, cocking his head to the side. "I'm not surprised. I never liked that little bastard."

Dad's remark startles a laugh out of me and Mom cuts him a dirty look. "George."

He shrugs. "Don't give me that look, Susanne. I'm just telling it how it is." Then, he focuses his gaze on me. "Have you found a lawyer yet?"

"Yes," I answer. "Rachel Lane from Matheson and Associates. She's working on a separation agreement now." I stall for a moment, eyeing them both. "I want to settle it quickly. The only thing I'm asking for is that he leaves my business alone."

"Don't short change yourself," Dad says. "You never know what could happen in the future, sweetie. You are entitled to half of everything."

I sigh. I knew Dad wouldn't just accept that part. "I know, but so is he. According to the lawyer, the courts will look at my potential earnings and could very well award him a share of my business, too. But the truth is, I don't want anything from him. I just want to be done and I don't want the reminders."

Both my parents are silent for a moment, both looking slightly shell-shocked and a little angry. I scan my menu and sip my water, all the while, wishing I had ordered a glass of wine (or two).

On the positive side, at least they're focused on Richard being a dick, rather than Joshua.

"Tell me more about this Joshua character," Mom says, eventually. "How long have you been in love with him?"

Or maybe they're not.

I let out a sharp laugh. "I'm in love with him?"

"Sweetheart." Mom makes a *tsk* sound. "Your eyes light up when you talk about him."

My eyes meet hers and she smiles a smile only a mother could. It's open and reassuring. It's the kind of smile that says *everything's going to be all right* and *we love you*, all wrapped together.

"We've been writing for four months now," I say hesitantly. "He tells me I'm beautiful every day, Mom. Every single day. He says that one day I'll see myself like he sees me. It's his mission."

Doubt nags at my chest as I say the words, tightening my throat.

It hurts.

Oh God, it hurts too fucking much.

The wounds that Richard inflicted on me run deep, an emotional scar left on my soul.

Tears sting my eyes, but I don't let them fall. He doesn't deserve any more of my tears, but I'm quivering, my body trembling from head to toe as I try to hold them in.

"Victoria, take a breath," Dad says, his voice stern, as he wraps an arm around my shoulder, pulling me into him.

I suck in a breath, then let it out, only to suck in another. "Sorry, it's just getting to be too much."

"Well," Dad says. "Clearly, it's over between you and Richard. I'll deal with him, honey. The threats will end. I promise you that."

"Dad ..."

"The point, honey," Mom says, cutting off my protest, "is that you see that it's over, and now you can move forward from here."

Dad nods. "As for this Joshua character—" he stalls, taking a deep breath. "Look, sweetheart, I'm not going to tell you how to live your life. If this is what you want, I'll support you, but be careful."

I let his words hang in the air for a moment, deciding that he's right. I need to be careful. "He wants me to move out there and I like the idea. I think, maybe for a few months, I could go and try it out. See how it goes."

"I think you should take a vacation," Mom says. "Go out there and spend some time with this man for a week or two. See how it goes before you decide to move there."

"Really?"

"Really," Dad surprisingly agrees. "I think it'll be good for you. Get away from all of this and give Richard some time to come to his senses."

I'm flabbergasted, glancing between them, certain I heard them wrong. But they're both smiling, both seemingly happy about this, and they genuinely look like they want me to go.

Parents, they say, know best, so who am I to argue?

"You know what," I say, smiling a watery smile. "I think I'll do that."

18

Road Trip

"Hey, what's good, sweetness?"

"Um, everything, I think."

My response makes Joshua laugh. "You only think?"

Sixty minutes ago, I finished packing my suitcases.

Thirty minutes ago, the movers loaded all my boxes and took them to Becca's place.

Twenty minutes ago, I approved the separation agreement and told my lawyer to send it to Richard.

Ten minutes ago, I booked my hotel.

Now, here I am, sitting on my bed, stressing a little that Joshua might not think this is such a hot idea.

So what's good? Everything, *I think.*

"Um, well, it's been an interesting day. I'm still at my house, but the movers just left with the last of my things.

They're meeting Becca at her place, and ..." I hesitate, chewing on my bottom lip. "I ... went to lunch with my parents."

"Good," he says, and he sounds like he means it. "I can't tell you how fucking glad I am that your shit is out of that place. How'd it go with your parents?"

"Surprisingly well. I told them about you."

"Oh yeah? What'd you tell them?"

I laugh. "I told them that I have a pen-pal who's in prison that I care for a lot."

"Really?" he asks. "You told them I'm in prison?"

"Yeah," I say, smiling at his surprise. "You were right. I needed to talk to them before *Dick* does."

"That's a big step," he says seriously.

"Yeah," I agree, and then shrug it off as I flop back onto the bed. "But I figure coming clean was the only way to make Richard's threats meaningless, but my dad wasn't too happy about it all."

"Okay," he says, then stalls, silence filling the line.

When he doesn't say anything else, I eventually say, "So, yeah, then I told them about Richard."

"And what'd you say?"

"That we're splitting up. I told them about all his threats and the affair. I told them about how he's been treating me since we got together. I told them everything."

More silence.

"And what did they have to say about it all?"

"Well," I pause, smiling to myself. "I'm kind of glad that

Richard's in Hawaii. My dad looked like he wanted to go kill him."

Joshua chuckles. "Yeah, I can imagine. I figured he'd be upset for all the nasty things Richard said and did to you."

"He was furious," I tell him. "He wanted to call him but I begged him not to. I don't need the headache that it would cause right now."

"Okay," he says. "Okay, well, what did they have to say about me? I'm kind of curious."

There's a hint of anxiety in his voice, a touch of fear, that has my leg bouncing, my nerves on hyper-alert. He's not the one who's supposed to be nervous. He's supposed to be the rock, strong and solid, nothing fazing him.

"Um, I don't really know how they feel about you to be honest," I say quietly. "They were both trying to be very open-minded and patient. They just want me to be happy." I stall for a moment, taking in a deep breath. "Um, I told them that I'm thinking about moving to Pennsylvania for a few months, just to sort of try it, live by you for a bit and see how it goes, and my mom suggested that I take a little road trip and come out for a week or two. Try it out and see what happens. You know, just while I'm working on the whole separation thing."

"Seriously?"

"Yeah," I say. "Seriously."

"That's fucking amazing," he says. "Are you going to come?"

His words instantly relax me. This is easy. Far easier

than I thought it was going to be. The truth is, I thought he might have an issue with me staying out there for a bit. "Do you want me to come?"

"Baby girl," he says, laughing. "Are you really asking me that? Of course I want you to come. I always want to see you. And it might be a good vacation for you, too. Get some time away from Richard."

"Yeah," I agree, glancing at my bags all packed and lined up by the bedroom door. "I'm kind of excited about it."

"I bet," he says. "You could relax or work, and we'd be able to see each other more often. And you know ..." he hesitates, clearing his throat. "If it'd make your parents feel better, I'd be happy to talk to them or even visit with them one day."

I laugh once, surprised. "Really?"

"Oh, definitely."

My mouth opens and closes a few times as I try to find a suitable response, but I'm not sure there is one. Although my parents took everything in stride today, they weren't overly happy about my choices.

"Maybe one day," I murmur back, my voice gentle and apologetic. "I don't think they're ready for that yet."

"Okay, there's no pressure. I completely understand. But you know, whenever they're ready, I'm here. I'm not going anywhere." He pauses. "So when are you coming?"

"Well, my bags are packed and I've booked the hotel already so I could leave whenever, I guess."

"Oh," he says, a hint of shock in his voice, "you're really serious about this. Will you be here tomorrow?"

"Yeah, I am," I say. "And I will, um, if you want me to be."

He hums into the phone. "I can't wait to hold you and kiss you again. I really miss you."

He misses me. Jesus, that sounds good. Feels good, too, and for half a second, I'm back in high school feeling all giddy, my belly full of butterflies. But the butterflies don't last nearly long enough, before anxiety takes hold of me, a feeling, one that squashes the butterflies and replaces them with knots.

"Do you think I'm crazy?" I blurt.

"No, baby, I think you're in love."

Sighing, I stand up, pacing across my room. "I kind of feel like all of this is a little crazy."

"You know what," he says quietly, "if someone would have told me a story like this and I'd never come to prison, I would have thought so, too. But I believe you came into my life for a reason. Don't you feel that way?"

"I do," I say, nodding my head, "but it still sounds crazy to me. All of it."

"Yeah?" he says, and laughs. "Well, baby, we can be crazy together."

His response makes me laugh. "Sounds like a plan."

"Good," he says, and I can hear the smile in his voice. He pauses, quiet for a moment, and then as he continues, his voice dips low. "So, baby girl, what are you wearing?"

Those words send excited tingles down my spine. I lick my lips. "Um, leggings and a tank top."

"And?" he pries. "What else?"

"A light blue bra and panties," I whisper, trying to keep the sudden arousal from showing in my voice.

"Are your panties see-through?"

"Mmhmm," I mumble, nodding. "Yes."

"So I could see your pussy lips," he says, his voice thick with lust. "I love how you wear my favorite color. It turns me on, you know that?"

"I was thinking about you when I bought them," I confess, embarrassment stirring inside of me. "I've bought a lot of blue since I met you."

"Really?" he asks, sounding genuinely shocked. "I love how caring you are. You always think about me. Is your pussy wet?"

"Yes," I whisper breathily. "It always is when I'm talking to you."

"Just thinking about that gets my dick hard, you know that?"

"Oh yeah?"

"Yeah, baby," he says. "I had a dream about you last night, actually."

I giggle, yep, giggle like a little girl. "Did you? What kind of a dream?"

"I was picturing I came in to our house and you were naked on the bed rubbing your clit. I looked down and your pussy was so wet, it got my dick so hard." He pauses, stalling for a moment. "Why don't you pull down your pants and your panties, baby? I want to make you come before you hit the road. Are your toys already packed?"

"Yeah," I say. "They're in my suitcase."

"Why don't you grab them. And get two of them this time."

My breath hitches. "Sure, Joshua. Whatever you want."

And I mean it. Whatever he wants.

19

Please, Please Tell Me Now

——————

Kissing Joshua is never going to get old.

His lips are on mine, demanding, yet soft, and one of his hands ... it's wrapped around my throat, squeezing just enough to send my heart racing and wetness gathering between my legs. The other is pressed firmly on my back, holding me as close as he can.

The way he's holding me ... I can't pull away, even if I wanted to.

I love it.

His thumb presses harder on my throat, and I gasp at the pressure, pressing myself tighter against him, as his tongue explores my mouth. Heat flares, pulsing through me. I need to get closer. I need more. I need ...

I let out a little whimper as his lips leave mine. He wraps

his arms around me, pulling me in tighter still for a quick hug. Time's up, but I'm not ready for the kiss to be over, not even close.

"Missed you, beautiful," he whispers against my ear. "So fucking glad you're here."

"Me, too," I say, squeezing him tight. "Missed you more than I thought possible."

And then he lets me go, taking a seat and tearing into his Swedish Fish. I teeter on my toes for a second, my knees weak, my head dizzy, before I take an ungraceful seat across from him.

I stare at him for a moment, watching him as he pops a candy into his mouth. He's enjoying it. I can see it on his face—in the brightness of his eyes, and in that smile.

Damn, I love that smile.

It reaches his eyes, crinkling the skin in the corners, flashing his straight white teeth.

It's pure, unrestrained, enjoyment.

"What are you looking so hard for?" he asks, his smile growing impossibly wider. "What are you trying to find?"

My cheeks flush. "Nothing. You just look ... you look so happy. What are you smiling so big about?"

Joshua shrugs and adjusts his position in his seat. "Nothing really. I had a really good day and I really loved that kiss."

"I loved it, too."

And I did.

I really, really did.

My pulse quickens just thinking about it.

"So ..." I say, glancing around. It's loud today, the visiting area crowded. "Why was your day so good?"

"I don't know." He shrugs again. "I slept really good, you're here." Another shrug. "Just really, really missed you, I guess. I don't know. Life's just going really good right now and ..." He stalls, and my eyes flick back to his, his voice drawing my attention back to him. His smile dims a little, although the happiness in his eyes looks as though it brightens. "Well, I also kind of got some news today."

"News?" I ask. "What kind of news?"

"The good kind," he says, leaning closer.

That's it.

That's all he tells me.

I purse my lips. "Well, what's the news?"

"Why are you so nosey today, my love?" he asks, regarding me peculiarly.

"Because that's just me," I say with a laugh. "I like being nosey."

"Let me just hold your hand real quick," Joshua says, reaching for my hand, taking it within his. "I need to touch you."

My belly flutters. Damn, how did I get so lucky? Richard would never ...

This man ...

"Tell me the news." I squeeze his hand, curiosity and

something else that I can't quite pinpoint, buzzing through my body. "What's going on? Please, please, tell me now."

He lifts a brow. "Do you really want to know?"

"Yes," I say with an exasperated laugh.

"Well," he says, digging into the balled up knot in the meaty part of my palm near my thumb, "today I went and saw the PRC board and they accepted me into work release."

I blink, stunned. "Really?"

I don't know what to say.

I didn't even know he was up for review yet.

"Yeah," he says. "It's going to be a big change for us, baby. Really big change."

"What's ..." My mind is racing; I don't even know what to ask. So many questions swarm my brain, so many thoughts ... "What's work release?"

My scattered response makes him laugh. "They're going to put me into a center with no fences. There will probably be like maybe two or three hundred inmates, so the living will be a lot better. And the best part is that I'll be able to get a regular job on the streets."

The excitement in his voice is contagious. I'm grinning—grinning so big that my cheeks hurt. "Oh my God, baby, that's so awesome."

"It's going to be great for us," he says. "I'll be able to save up some money for us for when I get out."

He's thinking about saving money for us?

Really?

His response knocks me off kilter, startling me by the passion and excitement in his voice. I'm stunned. Speechless. I'm …

I blink. "Really?"

"Yeah, so I'll be able to help," he says, raising his eyebrows at my expression. "It's really exciting, baby. It's like the best news I've ever had."

"I'm so happy for you."

"Baby," he says, his voice all smooth and soft. "You need to be happy for us."

Those words make me melt. If it weren't for the fact that I'm sitting, I'm pretty sure I'd be nothing more than a puddle on the floor. He begins rubbing my hand, putting just the right amount of pressure, breaking up all the knots, and just like the last time I was here, I feel as though we're alone.

I don't notice the other inmates or their families.

I don't see the guards.

It's just him and me and it's perfect.

And then, a sudden thought dawns on me. My smile falls. "Will this like … will we still be able to have visits?"

He grins at me. "Yeah, baby, and the visits even get better. We'll be able to eat outside during the summertime, and they cook out, too. Some of the locations have tracks, so we can walk around the track holding hands. Everything just gets better as the security level gets lower. Life's going to get so much easier."

I stare at him, dumbfounded. It sounds … amazing.

Better than amazing. I stammer and stutter for a moment, my thoughts coming faster than I can process them. When I finally get my voice to work, it's filled with excitement. "Oh my gosh. I don't even know what to say. This is just so cool."

He laughs. "You don't know what to say? With you, that doesn't happen too often, baby. You really like to talk."

I laugh, hard, and so does he. It's an awesome sound, packed full of raw energy.

It sounds like true happiness.

It makes my heart thunder in my chest.

"When does this all happen? When do you move? How long does it take?"

He shrugs and lets go of my hand, flipping his palm up for me. Instinctively, I dig in, massaging his palm. "It could take a week or it could take three. One day, they'll just tell me to pack up. Usually it's whenever a bed opens up, so I'm not sure which place I'll be going to yet. It might be one of a handful. I think there's about eight or nine of them in this state. But some of them even have things like fishing and boats you can go out on. It's pretty cool."

"Oh my God, I love fishing."

Joshua laughs. "Do you?"

I nod. "I used to fish all the time growing up."

"Really?" he says, his eyes widening. "That surprises me. I'm not much of a fisherman."

"My dad used to take me fishing all the time at our cottage. I loved it, loved being on the water, and anything

I caught my family would eat," I tell him. "I wouldn't eat it, because it was all slimy coming out of the water, and I just pictured the fish being slimy when I eat it. I just can't eat fish. The thought turns my stomach."

"Me neither," he says, his nose wrinkling in disgust. "Any time I smell fish, I think of nasty pussy."

A laugh bursts out of me. "God, what's with you and relating food to sexual things?"

"I can't help it," he says, smirking. "That's what I think of when I smell it. It's disgusting, just like mayo. That makes me think of come." He makes a face, and I laugh—hard. "But I don't even think I could kill a fish if I caught one. That's the problem, too. So I'm not really sure if I'm going to go fishing, but I might go out and swim."

"Nice," I say. "So, tell me more about the job, like what kind of work can you get?"

"Well, every center has different jobs," he says, pulling his hand away, and leaning back in his chair. "They have nurseries you can work for. One of the guys I know was working at Dominos, but he actually ended up getting fired and kicked back to the prison I'm at now."

I raise my eyebrows in question. "Why did he get fired?"

"He had his girlfriend come to work and they got caught having sex."

"Really?" My brows furrow. "Like at work?"

He lets out a sharp bark of laughter, his eyes dancing in amusement. "Yeah, at work. I guess he had his girlfriend show up, and his boss ended up reporting him. Going to a work release camp, you've got a lot more freedom, a job and a boss, and you don't have COs around. A lot of the guys end up getting kicked out for having cellphones, drugs, or they get caught having sex."

Huh. "Well, clearly I'll never be doing that with you at your job then."

A genuine look of surprise passes across his face. "Really?"

I nod. "Really."

"Baby," he says, "the point is not getting caught."

"I'm not going to risk you getting into trouble."

"Come on, baby," he coaxes. His voice is low and husky. "Haven't you wondered what it'd be like having me inside you?"

Yes! I think about it all the time and by the look he's giving me, so does he. He looks as though he wants to devour me.

"I think about it all the time." I pause, picking my words carefully. "But I don't think it's ..."

"So do I, beautiful," he says, pointedly cutting me off. "So if we could have the chance, I need to have you."

"Huh."

That's it.

That's all I've got.

Call me crazy, but even though I want him—like, really, really want him—fucking him in my car or in a bathroom at his work is not really what I had pictured for our first time.

Not even close.

He cocks an eyebrow. "What?"

"I don't know," I say, grabbing my untouched soda and taking a sip. "I just guess I pictured our first time together a little more romantic than in the parking lot of wherever you're working."

He regards me peculiarly for a beat. "I know, but think about how close we are now, then picture how much closer it'll bring us, having our bodies pressed together, our hearts beating fast, as we're one together—finally. It's going to bring us so much closer. I know it. Shit, just thinking about it is making me hard."

Heat rushes to my cheeks. "Will you stop it? You're making me blush."

"Everything makes you blush." Joshua chuckles. "Your cheeks are red pretty much all the time. I love it, though."

"They are not," I say, rolling my eyes.

"Oh, baby, yes they are," he says, his voice thick with amusement. "Your face gets red, then you look down. You can't even look up at me, then you start looking around and biting your bottom lip. It's so fucking cute. I love it."

I don't know what to say to that, so I just stare at him, my face burning up.

I take another sip of my soda.

Then I stare some more, trying really hard not to let my eyes fall to his crotch.

Another sip.

He stares right back.

"Why are you so quiet?" Joshua asks after a moment.

"I, uh, I ..." I purse my lips. "You have me all tongue-tied."

"Aw, so cute," he says, his brown eyes warming as he laughs. "You're adorable, baby." He pauses, leaning forward once more, watching me closely, so closely it's as though he's looking right into my soul. "So what are you thinking about?"

I roll my eyes. "Things that I shouldn't be thinking about."

"Tell me," he says.

I shake my head. "It's a secret."

He laughs yet again. "Oh, don't play hard to get now. Please tell me. Pretty please?"

I want to keep it to myself. I want to hold on to my thoughts tight. He just told me he wants to have sex with me at a job he doesn't even have yet, and I don't want to encourage the idea. But I can't make myself stop thinking about it when all I feel is elation at the thought that he wants me that much.

"I'm wondering if I'd ever have the guts to actually do that," I mutter. "To come to your job and have sex with you while you're on break. I don't know if I'd have the guts."

His expression shifts, the amusement fading when he grabs my hand. "You could wear one of those cute little dresses that you look gorgeous in. Don't wear any panties, and I can just lift it up and slide my hard cock inside you."

My heart's racing again, thumping in my chest. I watch his face as his gaze travels over me. I can see the want in his eyes. It's the same feeling warming my belly.

"And then we get caught," I grumble, "and you get sent back to where you're at now."

"Baby," he says quietly, "just one time, having the chance to make love to you would be worth it."

I stare at him as my heart does a funny little beat, skip, beat, beat, skip. I want to agree. Shit, I want to. Instead, I say, "Not quite sure I'd call that making love, baby."

He hums. "Whatever you want to call it, I want it so bad. It's all I think about every single day. You're all I want for the rest of my life."

20

I'm Moving Up, I Think

———————

The better part of Friday is spent in bed with my laptop. I'm on a roll, well over my word count goal for the day. It's a little after two o'clock in the afternoon when my phone starts ringing, a FaceTime request from Becca popping up on the screen. I swipe the screen, holding my phone up and centering my face for the camera. "Hey, Becca."

"Are you okay? I haven't heard from you in three days. *Three days!* I can't believe you left and you didn't call. I mean—did you forget about me? Are you ever coming back? I bet you already found an apartment and—"

"Whoa! Slow down," I interrupt her, closing my laptop and setting it aside. "It's all good. I'm fine. I made it to Pennsylvania and I'm at a hotel. Everything's good."

Becca drops her head, her eyes focusing on the floor.

———

She's at home. I see she's sitting on her bright red leather couch, and her hand's trembling slightly, the camera jiggling on her face.

"Hey, Becca, are you okay?" I ask gently, wishing I was there right now and I could wrap my arms around her.

"Yeah, I'm good." She lifts her head, flashing me a watery smile.

"Something's wrong," I say. "You're scattered. What are you hiding from me?"

"It's nothing I can't handle," she says, stretching her smile wider but it's still nowhere near as bright as her normal smile. "I'm sorry I freaked out a little. Nothing for you to worry about."

She looks tired, the dark circles under her eyes giving away how truly troubled she is.

"I'm sorry for not calling," I tell her. "I've been writing again and visiting Joshua, and yesterday I spent the day checking out the area, looking to see what kind of apartments are available."

She lifts a shoulder in a one-sided shrug. "No worries. I totally overreacted. It's just that ..." She hesitates, her eyes darting off to the side, before settling back on me, and then she lets out a sigh. "Look, I'm just worried about you. I'm sure Joshua is a good guy—" She laughs, shaking her head. "I mean aside from the whole being in prison thing, but I'm worried you're just ... rushing into something that might not be all that healthy."

I can't argue with that.

Guilty.

"I'm being careful," I tell her vaguely, because I'm not sure she'd understand exactly how much I already love the man.

Becca eyes me skeptically for a moment, then lets out a deep sigh. She doesn't argue my statement, but I know it doesn't reassure her. Switching subjects, I ask her how everything's going at work and how the weather's been at home.

She rambles on and on about the latest office drama, and I try to pay attention to the gossip, but it's lost on me. My mind's too full, too scattered, to really focus.

"Anyway, I should probably get back at it," Becca says. "Give me a call soon, okay?"

"Okay," I say. "I love you, Becca."

"Love you, too, babe."

Hanging up, I toss my phone down onto the bed, before getting up and shuffling into the bathroom. I turn on the shower, grabbing a towel while the water warms, and then pull off my sleep shirt, dropping it to the floor.

By four o'clock, I'm dressed in a jersey knit blue and gray striped dress and black leggings, sitting in front of the makeup mirror trying my damnedest to create a cat-eye look with my eye-liner all because Joshua mentioned he liked the look.

It's not working.

My lines are crooked, the angles way off.

Finally, giving up, I put on the usual basic eyeliner, grab

my purse and keys, and head out of the room, making my way to my car.

It only takes me fifteen minutes to get to the prison, and another five to make it through security. The visitation area is simmering with energy tonight. Nearly all the tables are filled, inmates and their loved ones smiling and laughing. Most of them are playing games: cards, Scrabble, Sorry, Monopoly. The prison seems to have an unlimited number of board games for the inmates and visitors to use.

I get drinks and snacks, before sitting at the short knee-high table. The plastic chair is crazy uncomfortable. I start fidgeting, tugging on my dress, as I wait for Joshua to appear in the glassed in room.

It's taking forever today.

I can feel my skin humming, my hands, every inch of me. I've never been this excited to see anyone in my life. Ever.

When he finally appears in the glassed in room, my heart stalls, and then thunders in my chest. He gives me a nod and a grin, watching me closely as he checks in at the guard's desk and then swaggers toward me. I don't wait for him to reach the table before I'm on my feet, and the moment he reaches me, his hands shoot out and grab me, pulling me into him.

He kisses me hard, his tongue invading my mouth urgently as his hands dig into my back, holding me as close as he can get me. My body heats instantly. I run my fingertips over his close cropped hair, as he practically inhales me, pressing my body closer until my hips are tight against his. My hand fists the back of his shirt, while my other hand grips his neck, nails digging into the skin. It's a frantic kiss. Desperate. It's ...

"You're fucking trouble, you know that?" he mumbles into my mouth as he digs into my hair, pulling me sharply away from his lips. He buries his face in my neck, nipping at my collarbone. "Every time I touch you I just want to bend you over and bury my dick in you."

I whimper, pulling against his hand, wanting his lips back on mine. "I'd let you. Anytime you want, I'd let you."

I don't even know what I'm saying, just mumbling and rambling, as I try to capture his lips once more. My skin is on fire; I'm so turned on.

"Beautiful," he says with a groan. "Got to let you go. They'll kick you out and take away our visits."

And then, he lets go.

I slump down in my seat, and pick up my drink, taking a long sip of the soda, trying to calm my overheated body. If someone had told me a year ago that I'd get this carried away with a kiss in such a public place, with so many people around, I would have laughed at them. But there's just something about Joshua—something so addictive.

"You want to know what I was thinking about on my way over here?" he says as he tears into his candy.

I shake my head, smiling as I set my drink down. "What?"

He pops a candy into his mouth. "That I can't wait until I have you on the back of my bike."

"You want me on the back of your bike?" I ask, my voice hesitant. Judging by his expression, this is a big deal, but I honestly don't understand why, and I was kind of thinking that maybe I'd get my own bike when he gets out.

"Yeah, baby," he says. "We could cruise down to the beach, I'd do some boogie-boarding while you tan. Then take a nice long ride. Wouldn't that be so much fun?"

"Yeah, I think so." I eye him seriously. "But, um, I wanted to get my own bike."

His brow furrows and he waves me off dismissively. "You're my ol' lady. You belong on the back of my bike."

I hesitate. "Did you just call me an old lady?"

He rolls his eyes and laughs, his expression showing his amusement before it falls away, turning serious. "No, baby, I'm not calling you old. You're my ol' lady, you're my girl."

"Huh." I don't know what to make of that. "I'm moving up, I think."

Joshua laughs, the amusement returning to his eyes. "Yeah, baby, you are. You're my ride or die bitch, the one I'm going to be with for the rest of my life."

"Really?" I ask. "Wait ... What does that even mean?"

He lets out another light laugh as he leans back in his chair, stretching. "It means you're going to be here for the good times and the bad times. You'll be here forever, just like you are now, at the worst point in my life."

I laugh. It's a nervous laugh, a happy laugh, and a freakin' terrified laugh. It's a mess.

Shit.

I'm a mess.

Dammit, he's adorable. His words make me feel all warm and fuzzy and ...

I grab my soda and take a sip. "What if I don't want to be your ol' lady? Do I have any say in this?"

"No, baby, not really," he says, reaching across the table and cupping my cheek, his voice playful as he adds, "Being my ol' lady is basically being my wife."

His wife? Really?

I blink a few times as his hand falls away. "Okay, but, if you ask me to marry you, I have the right to say no," I point out.

His brow furrows at my statement. "You belong to me, you know that, right?"

I roll my eyes, unable to stop myself from blushing as I take another sip from my soda. "Yeah."

"So you're already my property, what's wrong with being my ol' lady?" He sounds genuinely perplexed.

"I'm just saying ..." I sigh, dropping my eyes to the table. "What would happen if I said no? What if I don't want that? I'm not even divorced yet. I'm barely separated."

"Baby, look at me when you speak to me," he says, and when I don't raise my eyes, he reaches out a hand and cups my chin once again, this time forcing me to look back up at him. "Do you really believe you'd say no to me?"

"I didn't say that." I regard him curiously, wondering what exactly I was thinking when I let myself fall for a man like him. *I wasn't thinking, just feeling.* "I just want to know how all of this works. I don't know anything about bikers. I don't know anything about their policies or whatever."

Dropping my chin, he sticks another piece of candy in his mouth, chewing it slowly, before shrugging. "That's just how bikers are. I don't really know what to tell you, baby. You're just my ol' lady. I don't really need to ask you."

"Interesting."

"Why's that interesting, beautiful?"

"Is this really how it works?" I ask. "Some guy just says she's my ol' lady and that's it? There's no discussion? No one gives a shit whether she wants to be or not?"

Leaning back in his chair, he gets so quiet staring at me so hard that I get self-conscious, my face flushing under his scrutiny. Finally, he lets out a long sigh. "I can't tell you what other people do, but I can tell you what I'm doing. You're my ol' lady, so ..."

"So I'm supposed to just shut up and accept it." I scoff. "I don't think I'd actually make a very good ol' lady. I don't know how to shut up and I'm too nosey."

"That you are. You're nosey as hell, but I love that about you. It's not a bad thing." He laughs, amusement making his eyes shine. "But yeah, this is something you're supposed to just accept and be happy about. It's a pretty damn big compliment."

I start laughing and bring both of my hands up to my forehead. I don't know if it's from his statement or my nerves. It could be both.

"Damn, I love your laugh. It's so cute. It's one of those nervous laughs. You do it all the time."

"Um, thank you, I think."

"Why'd you give me a nervous laugh?" he asks, arching a questioning brow.

I shrug. "I don't know. I guess I just don't like this whole ol' lady thing."

Joshua closes his eyes and sighs heavily. When he opens them again, he leans forward and settles his elbows on his knees. "Would it make you feel better if I ask you?"

I don't know what I expect him to say, but it's not that. "Yes."

"Will you be my ol' lady, baby?"

My response comes immediately. "Yes."

Joshua laughs, shaking his head. "You can be so difficult about some things, but I fucking love you. Can't wait to see you in a 'property of' vest one day."

That statement makes me pause. It's one thing telling him I belong to him in private, but now I'm going to have to wear a vest advertising that I'm his property? Geez, what the hell have I signed up for here.

I shake my head. "I'm not sure I could wear a 'property of' vest."

"Oh you most certainly will," he says, matter-of-factly. "Why wouldn't you? Do you know how many women out there would suck and fuck anyone just to get a property vest? It's an honor and trust me, it doesn't have the meaning you think it does."

I arch a brow. "Please, enlighten me."

"Back in the days when all the clubs got together no one knew who the girls belonged to, which guys or club they were with. So they created the 'property of' vest so everyone knew who belonged where. It stopped other clubs from hitting on the girls that were taken, and stopped a lot of arguments and fights."

I blink. Okay, that's really not what I expected. "You're shitting me."

"Nope," he says. "I'm not shitting you."

Silence falls.

Joshua finishes off his candy as I sip my soda, trying—and failing—to wrap my head around this whole conversation. I'm still sipping my soda when he leans forward, taking one of my hands, drawing my attention to him.

"What are you thinking so hard about?"

"Does this new status mean you're going to answer all my questions now?"

He barks out a laugh. "We both know that's not going to happen. I'm sworn to secrecy on a lot of things, baby, but if it's something that I can tell you, then I'd tell you."

"I bet I could get your secrets out of you," I murmur, squeezing his hand.

Joshua shakes his head. "I'm like a vault."

"All vaults have keys."

"Not the good ones," he counters. "The good ones have

eye recognition. Unless you cut out one of my eyes, you're not getting in."

"Your eyes recognize mine."

His brow furrows. "What?"

"Your eyes recognize mine," I repeat. "You've never been in love like this before. I'm your key."

Joshua's face splits into a grin and he laughs—hard. "Cute. I love it when you play around."

21

You're Going to Miss Me

The next few weeks pass by in a blur. I work. I exercise. I search for apartments. And every chance I get, I'm at the prison, visiting Joshua—four days per week, and three hours per visit—and when I'm not there, we're on the phone.

It's been nearly three weeks since I arrived in Pennsylvania and every single day of it has been ... incredible.

I'm not sure what's happening at home, but my lawyer has kept me as updated as she can. The last update, Richard is reviewing the agreement with his lawyers—yes, lawyers, plural. Why he needs more than one is beyond me. It's not as though this is a complicated separation.

Actually, it's pretty simple. We have no children. I'm not asking for anything that isn't rightly mine, but whatever.

Hopefully, his team will talk some sense into him.

There still hasn't been any word on Joshua's move, but he swears the wait is normal, reminding me nearly every day that until a bed opens up, which could take weeks, he'll be stuck where he's at. And even though he doesn't know what part of the state he'll end up in until he's told to pack up, his insistence that I find a place and make the move right away has turned desperate. It's almost as though he thinks that if I don't have a place before I leave again that I'll never come back.

I don't know why he's stressing.

I'm sure he can see that I'm crazy about him.

There's nothing—absolutely nothing—that will keep me from coming back.

I'm thinking about all of these things, doing my makeup, and trying to decide how exactly I can reassure him when my phone rings.

Setting down my eyeliner, I pick up my phone and glance at the screen. Joshua. I answer it, bringing the phone to my ear, and I listen to the recording, waiting for my chance to accept the call.

"What's good, beautiful?" he says, as soon as the call clicks through.

I smile. Hearing him call me beautiful never gets old. "Just getting ready to come see you."

"Good," he says. "Have you finished your makeup yet?"

"Not yet. I just started, actually."

"You should do cat-eyes."

I frown, recalling the last time I gave that a try. "Um, I don't really know how to do cat-eyes. I can't get my lines straight."

"Could you try?" he asks softly. "I want to take pictures today and cat-eyes are sexy as fuck."

I laugh nervously, glancing at the clock. An hour and ten minutes until I'm supposed to be sitting across from him again. Maybe I could Google …

Just then, my phone beeps, another call coming through. I pull the phone away from my ear, quickly glancing at the screen. It's my lawyer.

"Hey, my lawyer's calling," I say as I bring the phone back to my ear. "I should really take it. Do you want to hold on or give me a call back?"

"I'll wait."

Pressing the hold and answer option on the screen, I answer the call tentatively. "Hello?"

"Mrs. Clarke, it's Rachel Lane calling."

"Hello," I say again. "How are you?"

"I'm doing well," she responds, her tone serious and all business. It should probably terrify me, but I only feel a slight chill. "I have some news for you. We've just received a response from your husband's lawyers."

"Okay?"

"The documents arrived this morning," she says. "I've

just completed my initial review, but it looks as though he's agreeing to all of your terms."

That surprises me, and I think she must be joking, but her tone is serious. I just can't imagine Richard agreeing, even if it's the smartest thing for him to do. "Really?"

"Yes," she says, "although he's added a nondisclosure agreement."

My eyes narrow at those words, wondering what the hell he's up to. "A nondisclosure agreement?"

"Yes. You'll need to come in and sign some documents. We can review the agreement when you come in."

"Of course," I say. "I'm still out of the country. Can this wait a week or two?"

"I wouldn't advise it. Until it's signed, your husband is free to make changes."

Her response makes me pause. "Okay, I guess I can leave tomorrow and drive straight through, but the soonest I can make it into the office would be Thursday morning. Will that work for you?"

"That's perfect," she says. "I'll schedule you in for ten o'clock Thursday morning then."

"Okay, see you then."

She hangs up and I tap the swap button on the screen, taking Joshua off hold. "Hey, baby. Sorry about that."

"Is everything okay?" he asks. "Is there any news?"

"Um, yeah," I say, and sigh. "Richard agreed to everything, but he wants me to sign a nondisclosure agreement."

"That's great, baby," he says. "So why do you sound so upset?"

"Yeah, it is great," I say. "But it means that I have to leave tomorrow."

"Why?"

"My lawyer said that I need to come in and sign everything right away. The sooner the better, so he can't make changes."

He's quiet for a moment, and when he speaks again, his voice is oddly detached. "It has to be done. I'll see you in a bit, okay? Love you."

He doesn't give me a chance to respond before a recording advises me that the caller has hung up. I stare at my phone for a beat, not sure what to make of his sudden change in attitude, and then I shake it off, bringing up the browser and searching for cat-eye tutorials.

****

"What's this for?" I ask, staring at the small yellow square of paper with the number forty-two scribbled on it.

"Hand it to the guard when you leave," he says. "I've got something waiting for you to pick up."

"Okay," I mutter, glancing up at him. "I'll do that."

He looks stunned. "Don't you want to know what it is?"

Yes, but I don't want to ask.

We're two hours into the last visit we're going to have for who knows how long and things are ... tense. We've barely talked, spending the whole time playing rummy, until moments ago, when he'd stood up and without saying a word, he'd walked away.

He wasn't gone long though, only a few minutes talking to the guards and filling out some kind of form, before returning with the scrap of paper.

I think he's stressed about me leaving.

Shit. *I'm* stressed about me leaving.

"Sure," I say, after a moment. "If you feel like telling me."

He nods, pulling the slip of paper from my hands and setting it on the table, and then takes both of my hands within his. "It's one of my T-shirts."

I let out a startled laugh. "You're giving me one of your T-shirts?"

"I am," he says, squeezing my hands. "You're going to miss me. I thought this may help."

I stare at him with shock. "I can't believe you're giving me one of your T-shirts."

"Why is that so hard to believe, beautiful?" he asks, lifting a questioning eyebrow.

I don't know what to say, don't know what to make of his gift. It's ... kind of perfect.

My eyes meet his and I stare at him.

He stares right back at me.

The silence is deafening.

Eventually, he lets out a dry laugh. "Not sure this is the reaction I was expecting."

"Sorry. I'm just ... I guess I just wasn't expecting it is all."

"I was watching TV the other day and there's this dating service where the men wear the T-shirt and it collects your pheromones," he explains. "Then the next day the women get to smell a whole bunch of shirts and the one that attracts them is the one that they pick." He stalls for a beat, a small grin appearing on his lips. "So I actually wore that T-shirt for you. You're going to miss me, so when you do, I thought you could wear it or just smell it to bring us a little bit closer."

My heart squeezes and my eyes prickle. Joshua watches me curiously, expectantly, waiting for my reaction. I gaze into his eyes, drinking in the emotion I see there.

Jesus, this man ... he's perfect.

"I don't want to leave." The words tumble from my lips in a whisper, a shuddering breath forced from my chest. "I'm not ready."

His eyes slowly close, and then open, eyeing me so hard my chest constricts under the pressure. "Promise me you're coming back," he says quietly. "Fucking promise me you'll come back."

"I promise."

"Don't say it unless you're going to follow-through."

"I promise," I say again. "I prom—"

I'm cut off mid-word. An inmate walks up to our table, stopping beside Joshua. "Time for pictures," he says.

Standing, Joshua reaches out a hand to me, pulling me from my chair, and twining his fingers with mine. "I love you, baby girl," he says as he tows me up to the front of the visiting room. "Come back to me soon, okay?"

"I will," I say, and I mean it. "I promise."

22

The Big Move

———

When I promised Joshua I'd be back soon, I hadn't realized that it would take me a little more than six months before I'd be able to make the move. I should have known. I should have guessed that settling up my affairs at home wouldn't be simple, but I'd been hopeful and really thought everything would go smoothly. And I might have also completely overlooked the fact that I couldn't just pick up and move to a new country. I really believed I'd be back with my man in just a few weeks, but as it turns out, applying for a VISA can be a lengthy process.

It's been the longest six months of my life.

After signing off on everything, Richard disappeared from my life. He hasn't tried to reach out, hasn't sent so much as a text. I don't know what his lawyers said to him to get him to walk away quietly, but whatever it was, I appreciate it.

He hasn't followed through on any of his threats, although I suspect that's only because I walked away without asking for anything. I suspect he's also concerned that if he tries to air my personal business, I might just turn around and do the same to him.

Or perhaps he's just come to the same conclusion as I have. There's a very real possibility that the *so-called* scandal may in fact help my business, rather than hinder it.

Whatever the cause for his silence, I'm thankful for it. Thankful that my life doesn't have the extra unneeded drama.

Joshua moved to a new institution and secured a job at a local diner. He's a dishwasher now, and although he hates the job, he's happy to be doing it. Happy to be out in the world, even if it is supervised.

We haven't seen each other since I left, my travel restricted while my VISA application was in process, and he stopped asking me when I'd be moving. He began calling less and less as work took over his life, averaging only two calls per day. It's taken a toll on our relationship. We no longer have time to chat about all the little random things we used to, only focusing on the major things happening in our day-to-day lives.

He reassures me daily, though. Telling me how different it'll be when I'm finally there with him. I can stop by at the restaurant while he's working, and visit him four nights a week at the prison. I honestly cannot wait until I can feel his arms around me again.

My parents have been nothing but supportive, although I can tell they're still not one-hundred percent on board with my decision to move to the U.S. Even so, they helped me secure an apartment and helped me through the customs nightmare of importing all my belongings, including my truck. I'd probably still be stuck on the Canadian side of the border if it weren't for them.

But it was Becca who kept me sane. She's been my rock, and she's thought of everything. She rented the U-Haul trailer, ordered furniture, and coordinated the deliveries. She even worked with the Ford dealer, trading in my car for the F-150 I'd always wanted.

In a nutshell, my best friend is a freakin' rock star.

We're standing outside my new apartment, my keys in hand, eyeing the overfull U-Haul trailer. I still can't believe that Becca took time off work to help me with my move, but she did, and I don't think she'll ever fully realize how much I appreciate it. I can't really remember the last time I felt this happy ... this giddy.

"You know," Becca says around a yawn as she looks over all the boxes, "maybe we should run over to a Walmart and get one of those dolly things."

I can tell by the look on her face she doesn't really like the idea. It's early, just barely nine o'clock in the morning. We'd stopped over in Massachusetts last night, leaving before daybreak and only stopping for gas during the six-and-a-half-hour drive. We're both feeling it. But the sun is out now and the air is starting to warm, the typical May temperature creeping in.

Glancing across the parking lot to my first floor unit, I say, "We could just back up the truck to the patio door and unload it that way."

"Do you know how to back this thing up?"

I shake my head. "Nope, but it can't be that hard."

She laughs, casting me an amusing look as I close up the trailer doors and stroll over to the driver's side of the truck. I hop in, starting it up. Dierks Bentley's *Drunk On a Plane* pours out of the speakers. As I slip the truck into gear, my phone rings. Sighing, I pull it out of my pocket, turning down the radio and sliding the truck back into park, glancing at the screen and spotting Joshua's number popping up there. I answer it, drumming my fingernails on the steering wheel as I wait to accept the call.

"Hey, baby," he says once the call connects. "Are you at the apartment yet?"

"Yup," I say. "I just got my keys and we're about to find out if I have the skills to back the truck and trailer up to the patio door, or if I'm going to have to run out and buy a dolly."

He laughs. "Just sit tight. Some of my guys are on the way over to give you a hand. They'll be there any second, okay?"

His words make me stall. "I … uh … I don't think … I'm not really comfortable with that."

And I'm really not.

Not only am I not ready to meet his, um, kind of *friends*, but I seriously don't want to do it dressed in a tracksuit. Sure, it's a stylish hot pink Juicy Couture tracksuit, but it's still a tracksuit. My makeup isn't done. My hair is tied up in a frizzy ponytail. And I've been driving for hours.

"Baby," he says, drawing out the word. "You're part of my world now, part of my family. We take care of our own."

I bite my bottom lip. I don't know what to say. I want to argue with him, but I know it'll be a useless effort. He's using that tone. It's the one that tells me that this isn't something that's up for discussion.

"Look, baby, I've got to go," he says when I don't respond. "Don't worry your pretty little heart. It's going to be fine. I'll see you tonight, okay?"

"Okay," I mumble, nodding my head. "See you tonight."

"Okay, good," he says, hesitating as though he doesn't really want to hang up. "Love you, baby girl."

"Love you, too."

I hang up, stuffing my phone back in my pocket. I can already hear the rumble of Harleys approaching as I pop my door open, and slide back out of the truck. I peek over at Becca. She's staring at me, one eyebrow arched in question. "Do you want me to give it a shot?"

I shake my head. "Joshua is sending some friends over to help."

Her eyes widen. "Really? Who?"

I don't get a chance to answer her before the parking lot is filled with the roar of bikes as two file in, so I shrug helplessly, pointing. "Them."

Becca's gaze shifts to the motorcycles, and then she looks at me, horrified. "Are you sure?"

"Pretty sure." I hesitate, taking in the colors on the back of their vests as they park. "They're wearing his club colors."

"No way," she says. "Babe, this is ... this is kind of scary."

"Yeah," I mumble, smoothing back some loose frizzy strands of hair. "Maybe, but he wouldn't send them if it wasn't safe."

Becca moves in closer to me, linking her arm through mine as the men park their bikes and come toward us, and I take a moment to control my facial expression, fiddling with my phone in my pocket. I don't want them to see that their presence is freaking me out a little.

These men are not the kind of men I'd normally speak to.

No. These are the kind of men I'd typically avoid.

They're big and tattooed and scary.

They stop in front of us, neither of them smiling.

"Victoria?" the really big man on the right asks. At least six-foot-two, his light brown eyes look down at me, making me feel super-small.

"Um, yeah, that's me," I say as my stomach becomes one big knot because neither of them look all that impressed or happy to be here. They're young, I think. Maybe thirty, though no more than thirty-five.

He gives me a slow once over, then nods once. "Swag's told us a lot about you," he says, offering his hand. "I'm Chow."

"Hi," I say, taking his hand and shaking it, blinking. "Um, who's Swag?"

He gives me a peculiar look, and then laughs—hard. "He's your man." Another loud laugh falls from him. "Knew he was trying to shelter you, but shit ... He didn't even tell you his nickname?"

I shake my head. "Why do you call him Swag?"

"Because," the other one says, smiling warmly, "he's got a lot of swagger." He sticks out his hand to me, and I accept it, shaking it quickly. "I'm Ali."

"Good to meet you both."

Ali cocks an eyebrow, his gaze shifting to Becca. "And who might you be?"

"Oh, uh, yeah." I glance at her, shaking my arm a little as her grip tightens on me. "This is Becca."

A look of amusement flashes across his face as he watches her press closer to me. "Right, the best friend."

Feeling awkward, I look away from them glancing around the parking lot, my gaze settling on my truck. "So, um, I know Joshua sent you guys to help me out, but I'm—"

"Don't bother," Chow says, stopping me mid-sentence. "We're not leaving till you're all settled in and enough of your neighbors know who you belong to."

His dead serious tone makes me laugh. "You can't be serious."

"Shit, your smile's cute," he says. "Like a little chipmunk."

I scrunch up my nose, trying hard not to smile. Becca giggles, catching my expression.

"Oh, come on," she says, nudging me with her elbow. "He's kind of right."

"Is that your truck, Chipmunk?" Chow asks, smirking.

I grit my teeth at the nickname, nodding. "Yeah, that's my truck."

"Hand over your keys," he says. "We'll finish this up for you."

"I'm not just giving you my keys," I say incredulously. "I don't even know you."

"Don't be a bitch and give me your keys," Chow snaps. "We're here to help."

My eyes widen, and I open and then close my mouth when nothing comes out. A ball of nervous energy fires up in my belly as he glares at me. *Will you please not call me a bitch, asshole?* I want to yell it. Scream it, really.

But I don't.

I don't get a chance to.

"They're in the ignition," Becca mumbles, and with

another hard glare, both bikers turn away from me and go to my truck.

****

The day drags, each minute feeling like an hour, each hour feeling like a whole day. The guys get all my things unloaded and return the U-Haul trailer. They even set up my bed, coffee table, and new bookshelves when the furniture is delivered.

They haven't left yet, and they haven't warmed up to me either, but I can hear Becca through the door, laughing and joking around with them.

I guess they can't be that bad, but the truth is, I don't really care.

I'm a bundle of nerves.

I'm full of excitement.

I've never been this nervous or this excited in my life.

I have ten minutes before I have to leave for the prison. I've showered and shaved and brushed my teeth. My hair is done, so is my makeup, the cat-eyes that Joshua likes damn near perfect, but I can't seem to make myself get dressed.

I'm sitting on my new bed wearing nothing but my bra and panties, knees pulled up to my chest and my arms wrapped around them, staring down at the outfit laid out beside me. It's perfect, red skintight jeans that hug my new curves, a black low-cut top, and a brand new pair of red heels.

I'm anxious to see him, but I'm nervous about it. Six months is a long time to go without seeing each other. I'm down thirty-four pounds since the last time I saw him. What if I've lost too much weight? What if he doesn't like my smaller, but rounder, ass? What if …

When someone pounds on my door, I glance up, calling out, "Just a minute."

Jumping up, I grab a towel, wrapping it around myself, before rushing over to the door, and yanking it open. I expect to find Becca standing at the other side, but instead, I find Ali.

"Fuck, Chipmunk," he says, eyeing me from head to toe. "You've got to get out of here. Swag's going to be pissed if you're late."

I glare at him, feeling myself starting to panic. I open my mouth, then close it, trying to calm myself but it doesn't work, and I snap, "I don't care if he gets pissed."

"Bitch, watch your tone," he says, his voice dropping low. "Don't yell at me because you're running late."

I cringe. God, I don't think I'll ever get used to being called *bitch.*

"I'm sorry. I'm a little nervous," I tell him, my eyes watering as I force a half smile. "It's just … what if—"

"Dry those tears up and get dressed," he says, cutting me short. "You've got five minutes to get your ass out of here."

His tone is sharp and it's not a request. It's a demand. My skin prickles as he gives me a hard look, before he turns away, shutting the door behind him.

I get dressed in record time.

Dropping the towel, I throw on my jeans and top, and slip on my heels, in under sixty seconds.

When I emerge from the bedroom, Chow is gone, I notice, and Becca is sitting on the couch, drinking a beer with Ali. My gut instinct is to ask him to leave, because Becca is seriously not capable of handling his kind of trouble, but I manage to swallow it down. I've already snapped at him once today, and I'm not sure I want to try my luck for the second time.

I get to the prison with three minutes to spare, and as I pull up and park, I don't think I can possibly get any more nervous, but my anxiety builds as I go through security, the guards putting me on edge as they scrutinize my identification and my outfit. I'm suddenly worried that I missed some rule about skinny jeans and they're going to turn me away. By the time I'm through the metal detector, my heart is racing and I'm having a hard time catching my breath.

The work release institution is set up differently. Instead of walking back outside and through some gates, I'm directed to a door off to my left. I walk into a small corridor and step up to the next door, waiting for the buzzing of the locks as the sign directs, and then I step up to the guard's desk.

They place me at table twenty-eight, which is at the very back of the room, right beside the inmate washrooms. I try to keep myself busy while I wait for Joshua, going to the vending machines, getting us drinks and his Swedish Fish. Then making my way back up to the guard's desk, and getting a deck of cards before finally taking a seat.

And then, I fidget.

And I stress.

And I watch the door.

The seconds tick by, turning into minutes, and my belly twists and turns, but when that door finally opens and my eyes meet his, I swear to God, all of my anxiety just ... disappears.

He has a huge smile splitting his lips and he's staring at me as though I'm the only person in the room. It's his smile that gets me to my feet, and I'm standing at the side of our table by the time he reaches me.

"Shit, baby, you look fucking amazing," he says. "Missed you so fucking much."

And then he pulls me into his arms and his lips find mine and I instantly feel at home.

23

You Want Me to Tattoo That Where?

It's been fifteen minutes and Joshua hasn't stopped staring at me.

He watched me as I sat down across from him, and his eyes followed me as I went back up to the vending machines. They were stuck on me when I stopped at the microwave, heating up a bacon cheeseburger for him, and they never left me as I brought it back to the table, opening up the ketchup and smothering it on his food. They stayed on me while he devoured his meal, and he was still staring when I collected all the garbage and threw it out.

Now I'm sitting across the table from him, leaning forward with my forearms pressed against the plastic top. His thumbs are stuck within my grip, his fingers wrapped around my hands, and his eyes, well, his eyes are still glued to me.

"Baby, you've got to stop staring so hard," I mumble, my eyes dropping down to the table. "It's making me a little … uncomfortable."

"Can't help it," he says, releasing one of my hands and reaching over, tapping my chin with a finger, bringing my gaze back to his. "You look fucking amazing. How much weight did you lose?"

"Thirty-four pounds," I say, smiling softly.

He smiles back at me and slips his hand back in mine. "Baby girl, I'm so proud of you. All that hard work paid off. Why didn't you tell me you've been doing so good?"

"Because," I swallow, because it's still hard for me to talk about my weight, "I wanted to surprise you, then I started to worry I was losing too much and that my ass was getting—"

"You look fucking fantastic," he says matter-of-factly, cutting me off. "It's gotten bigger, rounder—" He stalls, his eyes falling to my hips. "It's sitting up nice and high now, baby, and when you walk … shit, it fucking shakes perfectly. Your face has thinned out, your arms, throughout your whole body. I mean, wow. You look sexy as fuck."

Feeling my face heat, I quickly say, "Thank you for the workouts. I guess they really helped."

"I'm so proud of you for sticking with it, baby," he says, and he means it. I can see it in his eyes, hear it in his voice.

"Thank you."

He grins at me, and damn I love that grin. It makes my heart ache in a wonderful kind of way. I smile back. I can't help it. I never thought having the man I love appreciate all the effort that goes into losing the weight would feel so good.

But it does.

It feels fan-freakin'-tastic.

"So," he says, but then pauses, taking a breath. "Tell me, how did the move go?"

"You called them, didn't you?" I don't know why I ask the question, but it's out of my mouth before I can stop it.

He nods, amusement sparking in his eyes. "Yep, but I'd like you to tell me about it."

"Well," I start, a small, fake laugh falling out, as I try to find the words that might smooth everything over. "I think it went pretty well overall. Each of them only called me a bitch once throughout the entire day, so I think that might be considered a success."

Fortunately, he finds this amusing.

"I heard," Joshua says with a laugh, but when he continues, his voice is serious. "I also heard you got all teary-eyed and opened your bedroom door for Ali wearing only a fucking towel."

His tone makes me cringe and I try to pull my hands away, but he holds them fast. "I assumed it was Becca."

"That shit better not happen again," he says firmly.

"You're mine. The only man that gets to see you naked is me. We on the same page?"

"I wasn't naked."

He narrows his eyes. "Are we on the same page?"

I nod. There's no point in arguing. Honestly, if I hadn't been so damn stressed, I probably would have shut the door in Ali's face as soon as I saw him.

I guess my nod isn't enough, because Joshua tightens his grip on my hands and says, "Give me the words."

I hesitate. I want to say something snarky, but with the way he's looking at me, his expression serious and a little stormy, instinct tells me not to. "We're on the same page."

He grins, loosening up on my hands so I can pull them free. I take them back quickly, picking up my soda and taking a sip.

"I'm really glad you made the move, baby. So fucking glad you believe in us enough to be here, living close to me."

I set down my soda, my smile fading, but my happiness soars. "Me, too, Joshua. I'm really fucking glad I'm here."

****

Three hours later, we're playing cards, and Joshua is abnormally quiet, looking lost in thought. I lay down yet another rummy, and he, as always, picks up the card and places it back in my hand, gesturing for me to try again.

At least he's focused on the cards.

"You know," I say, pursing my lips, "we don't keep score. It doesn't really matter if I make mistakes."

"I know," he says. "But I like the look on your face whenever you win a hand. It's so fucking cute."

I can't help but grin at that. This man ... he makes me feel so special, so cherished. "Okay, baby."

He hums. "Love that smile, too. And the guys are right, you look like a cute little chipmunk when you show your real smile."

I laugh. It's an awkward, loud laugh. "Thank you, I think."

Joshua smiles, but he doesn't say anything more, focusing back on his hand. He picks up a card, glances at it, and then discards it, his smile fading.

I watch him for a moment, a small knot forming in my stomach as I reach for a card, picking it up and stuffing it into my hand, discarding another. His brow furrows, small frown lines forming between his eyes.

"Is everything all right?" I ask.

He looks up at me, shooting another quick smile that doesn't last nearly long enough. "Of course. Why wouldn't it be?"

I shrug. "I don't know. You're just ... quiet."

"I was just thinking that maybe we could come to a compromise on something." He shrugs. "Just trying to figure out how to propose it, is all."

"Compromise on what?" I ask, squirming in my chair, feeling suddenly uncomfortable.

"I know you said you really didn't like the idea of a 'property of' vest," he says, his gaze focused on his cards. "So I've got an idea that I think is even better, and it'd mean the world to me."

His words send a tingle spreading throughout my belly, and I try—unsuccessfully—to quash it. I've never really liked the whole property term. I'm not a feminist by any means, but really, being called property is just kind of … insulting. But when I hear Joshua use it toward me, it makes me feel giddy.

It's confusing.

It's messed up.

"Um, okay …"

He tosses his cards down, leaning back in his chair. "I'd like you to get a 'property of' tattoo right on the side of your ass."

A tattoo?

Really?

I don't know what to say.

He flexes his hands on his knees as though he's anxious for my answer, but once again, I'm sitting here, speechless, watching him as he watches me right back.

"It would mean the world to me," he says after a beat, softening his voice.

I try to ignore the fresh wave of delightful little tingles his words cause in my belly, and really think about what he's asked, but I can't. Not even a little. My body is alive with chills and tingles.

Oh, God, what's wrong with me?

This should not be turning me on and twisting me up.

It should not.

My heart is hammering, and when I speak, my voice is breathless. "You want me to tattoo that where?"

He smirks at me. *He freakin' smirks!*

Damn him, he knows exactly what he's doing to me.

"Baby, don't you think a tattoo right on the side of your hip, running across your ass cheek would be fucking hot?" he asks, cocking an eyebrow. "You could do it just like a vest, the 'property' would be arched, 'of' in the center, then below that would be my initials. It would look so sexy on you and I figured, since it'll be covered all the time, you might like it a bit more than the vest."

I look at him in confusion, because, well, how is this a compromise? "I'm not quite sure how permanent ink is a compromise from a removable vest."

"Well, it's not," he says, still smirking at me. "Not really, but you know we're going to spend the rest of our lives together, right?"

Ugh, I want to kiss that knowing smirk right off his lips. I hate the stupid rules. Hate that I can't kiss him, hug him, or have any other contact than simple handholding.

It sucks.

It sucks so freakin' hard.

Since I can't kiss him, I answer him honestly. "I hope so."

"This means more to me than a ring," he murmurs, his

eyes tender. "I know I'm going to spend the rest of my life with you and this tattoo is saying that this, what we have here, is forever. You mean the world to me, so of course if you got 'property of' with my initials, showing that you're in this for the rest of our lives, it would mean the world to me, too."

"Whoa, ease up on the sales pitch, baby," I laughingly tell him, because I'm not sure how to react to this.

Silence.

The tenderness leaks away from Joshua's eyes and his expression blanks, not betraying any emotion.

"It's not a sales pitch, Victoria," he says eventually, sounding truly agitated. He leans forward, reaching for my hands, twining his fingers through mine. "This is a tattoo I've always wanted my wife to get. I've never had a wife, and I know you're going to be it. Just think about it, okay? There's no pressure whatsoever. I don't ever want you to feel pressured. I just want you to think about it."

"You want me to be your wife?" I ask disbelievingly. I know he's said it before, but still, it's hard to believe.

"Yeah, baby, I do," he says. "Every time I look in your eyes, I know I'm going to spend the rest of my life with you. You're my everything, my world."

"Five minutes." The voice startles me so much that I jump, nearly falling off my chair as I turn toward it, spotting a CO chuckling at my reaction. "Sorry to scare you, ma'am."

I nod to him, my face flushing hot as he walks away. I

groan and hide my face in my hands, but after a moment, both Joshua and I burst out laughing about it.

I watch him, loving the deep timbre of his laugh and the way his eyes crinkle when he smiles, and for the life of me, at this moment I can't remember why I'd been so scared to see him again.

"Why do you always leave these earth shattering conversations to the last few minutes?" I ask as I catch my breath. "You never give me the chance to talk it out."

He grins. "Baby, this isn't earth shattering. It's just a tattoo."

"It's a tattoo that means the world to you," I point out. "That makes it kind of earth shattering."

"I'll tell you what," he says. "We've only got a couple minutes left, so why don't we just enjoy each other real quick, and I'll give you a call when you leave. We can talk about it as much as you need."

I raise a questioning eyebrow. "Promise?"

"I promise," he says, studying me intently. "I always want to know what you're thinking and how you're feeling. I swear to you, baby girl, your thoughts really matter to me."

Emotion, happiness and love and something else that I can't quite decipher, clogs up my throat. I look at him, nodding my head, and mouthing the word, "Okay."

24

Tattoos, Restrooms, and Duffle Bags

Tattoos on the ass take forever to heal.

I'm standing in my bedroom, the banded bottom of my black mini cold shoulder dress pulled up over my hips, staring at the old English lettering stretching across my right ass cheek. It's been sixteen days since I got the new ink, and it's still peeling.

It looks good. Clean lines. Bold lettering. My favorite part though, the small watercolor butterfly hanging off the 'L'. Each time I look at it, my heart aches in a wonderfully delicious sort of way. I never thought a tattoo could make me feel this ... special.

Grabbing my moisturizer, I pump out a generous glob, and massage it into my skin, before pulling my dress back down. I fluff up my hair, and then grab my eyeliner, touching up my waterline, when the door flings open and Becca walks in. I glance that way, taking in her cautious expression as she flops down on my bed. "I thought you were seeing Joshua today."

"I am."

"They're not going to let you in wearing that," she says, frowning. "It's showing shoulder."

"I'm not going to the prison." I hesitate. "I'm going to the diner."

She blinks at me. "For real?"

"Yup."

She blinks again. "Seriously?"

"Seriously."

She rolls her eyes, her expression showing that she thinks I'm kidding, before something clicks and her eyes widen. "Shit, you're serious," she says. "Babe, are you ready for this?"

I shrug. "If he wasn't in prison, it would have happened months ago."

"Yeah, but he could get in serious shit," she counters.

That he could.

Becca stares at me waiting for some kind of response as I try to get my thoughts together and figure out what to tell her. "It's a risk he's willing to take."

"I bet he is," she says seriously. "But is it one you're willing to take?"

Her knowing tone does something to my insides that I don't like. I bristle. I want to tell her that I'm a risk taker, that all I've been doing since I met him is take risk after risk, but I know that's just my insecurities pushing their way out. So I just shrug, because the truth is, I'm really not sure that I am willing to take the risk.

Becca eyes me for a moment, looking at me as though she's debating whether or not to push the topic, but thankfully she doesn't. "So, I was thinking I'd stay another week or two. Just to make sure you're okay here."

"Really?" I ask, my eyes widening. "Wait. What about work? Can you afford to take that much time off?"

"It's all good," she says, waving off my questions. "I've got like four more weeks of vacation banked up."

I grin, and so does she.

Damn, I love my best friend.

****

Twenty-nine minutes later, I'm staring at my reflection in the rearview mirror, trying and failing to convince myself that I can do this.

Resting my head on the steering wheel, I resist the urge to pound my head against it. I'm sitting in the parking lot outside the small family-owned diner that Joshua works at. He's been talking about me meeting him here for days now. He said that his boss leaves daily at two o'clock in the afternoon to go to the bank, and that he's always gone for a least an hour. It's been the same routine every single day since he started.

He's confident that we won't get caught.

Me, on the other hand, I'm not so sure.

And yet, here I am, sitting in the parking lot. It's six minutes after two, and his boss's car is gone. My truck is off, and I'm trying to build up the nerve to actually get out.

I take a deep breath, and then another, before I finally open the door and get out. Shutting the door, I look across the parking lot. The restaurant is busy, only a handful of spots left.

"This is a bad idea," I whisper as I start toward the door, slowly placing one foot in front of the other.

"This is a fucking great idea," a deep voice rumbles from beside me. I jump, spinning around as Joshua steps away from the dumpster and toward me. He closes the distance between us, placing a quick kiss on my lips, before taking my hand.

"Sorry," I say quietly against his lips. "I didn't see you."

"I was watching you, beautiful," he says. "Didn't think you were going to get out of that truck. I was about to come over when you finally did."

Shit. Seriously?

He was watching me?

How the hell didn't I notice him?

He must see the question painted on my face because he laughs and continues, "You had your head down on the steering wheel."

"Oh, right."

That's it.

That's all I can say.

"Come on, baby," he says, tugging on my hand. "Let's go inside."

I go with him.

Everything in my body tells me not to, but still, I go with him.

I'm pretty sure I'd follow this man anywhere—everywhere.

He lets go of my hand when we reach the door, and I'm shaking, trembling right down to my toes. He opens it, ushering me through, as he leans in to me, whispering and pointing, "Go on to the restroom right over there. I'll follow you in just a minute."

I hesitate before slowly nodding. "Okay."

A hint of a smile takes over his face as I turn to walk away. I should be worried. God, who am I kidding? I am worried, but it doesn't stop me from walking down the short hallway and slipping into the single stall women's restroom.

And then I wait.

And I wait.

And I wait some more.

Seconds turn into minutes.

Two, three, five.

I try not to think about the fact that I'm in a public restroom, about to have sex with the man of my dreams for the first time.

At least it's a clean restroom.

I wash my hands, and run my fingers through my hair. I fidget with my dress, smoothing and straightening it, and then I watch the door.

And watch.

And watch.

And then it finally opens, and Joshua steps in, locking it behind him. He grins at me, a grin that has me both anxious and melting at the same time. "Turn around, baby," he says, his voice husky. "I want to see that sexy ass of yours."

My heart hammers in my chest as I nod, slowly turning around. As soon as I do, his hands are at the hem of my dress, shoving it up to my waist.

"No panties." He hums his approval, then falls silent. I struggle to keep myself still under his scrutiny. When he speaks again, his finger trailing over my new ink, his voice is so low I almost miss it. "Perfect, just like you."

I bite my lip, looking back at him. God, he looks good. He smells good, too. The fresh scent of dish soap clinging to him. "I don't think this is a good idea."

"You've got nothing to be nervous about," he says. "I'm not going to do anything you don't want to do."

"It's not that," I mutter, ducking my head, suddenly glad my back is to him. "I want to. It's just that ... well, this is ... real. It's not over the phone. It's real and well, what if it's not, I mean ... I'm not good?"

He lets out a loud bark of laughter. "Haven't been inside

a woman in a very long time, beautiful. If anyone should be worried, it's me."

"Don't laugh at me," I whisper. "This isn't funny."

Joshua cups my chin with his hand so I have no choice but to look back at him, and his other hand wraps around my waist, pulling my bare bottom flush against his jeans. He leans in, brushing his lips across mine, and I let out a shuddering breath. Letting go of my chin, his hand wraps around my hair, pulling tightly and arching my neck.

And then his lips are on my throat, and he's murmuring words that I assume are supposed to be soothing, but I can't make them out over the need buzzing through me. I gasp as his hand travels lower, his finger sliding between my folds, and he groans, "You're already so fucking wet."

His dick is already hard, too. I can feel his length straining against his jeans, pressing against my ass. It sends a thrill soaring through me. I reach back blindly, my hands slipping between us, and I work to undo his jeans as his finger circles my clit.

I let out a moan as he slides two fingers inside me, pumping them in and out a few times. He kisses and licks and nips at my neck. And suddenly, I'm caught in a whirlwind of sensations, and I don't ever want to touch the ground.

Finally freeing his button, I work my hand into his open jeans. It makes my heart race faster than before. I grasp his length, stroking it, loving the feel of his silky skin in my hand.

"Baby, put your hands on the wall," he says. "I need to get inside you."

He doesn't have to ask me twice. I do as he says instantly, taking a step forward, placing my hands on the wall.

As soon as my hands are in place, I glance back, watching him watch me as he pulls down his jeans and boxers. I don't get a chance to admire him before he's behind me, one of his hands on my hip, pulling my ass out toward him. He rubs the head of his cock against my entrance, sending tingles through my body.

"Your pussy feels so good," he says as he pushes into me for the first time.

I want to tell him that his cock feels so good, too, but I can't. The words won't come out around the sudden moan that fills my throat.

Joshua pulls out, before pushing back in again, moving slowly, and I'm thankful for the moment to catch my breath.

The breath doesn't last long.

Joshua thrusts into me again—hard. So hard that it knocks the breath from my chest. I gasp, my hands slipping on the wall as his grip on my hips becomes tighter. And when one of his hands slips down, his finger circling my clit, my entire body shudders. I try to keep it quiet, I really, really do, but with each deliciously hard thrust the sounds just pour out of me. I'm moaning. I'm gasping. The noises mixing together, sounding far too loud, but I just can't swallow them down.

I can already feel it. My body tightening, the warmth and pressure building, and I cry out as my orgasm explodes inside of me. I can feel myself squeezing around his dick, my muscles contracting and releasing, and I think it sends him over the edge, because he groans and thrusts back into me hard, before stilling, his fingertips tightening on my hip.

I feel his breath panting against my neck, and then I feel his lips there. "Fucking love you, baby girl."

"I love you, too."

He stays inside me for a moment, his arms wrapping around me, his chest pressed against my back, but all too soon, he withdraws from my body.

I instantly feel empty.

Joshua uses the toilet, as I clean myself up and try to straighten my appearance. He doesn't say anything, and I don't either, though the silence doesn't surprise me. It's always hard saying goodbye, though this time it feels even harder.

Sex, even restroom sex, changed something in me.

I want to tell him I don't want to leave. I want to let him know I wish he was coming home with me. I want him to know that I already miss his touch.

But mostly, I want him to know that I need him.

But I keep my mouth shut. I have to. The last thing I

want to do is make him remember that at the end of the day, he's not coming home to me.

No, at the end of the day he's going back to a prison.

When he's finished, he steps over to me, pulling me into his arms, smiling down at me. "Stop fidgeting, baby. The *just fucked* look you've got going on looks sexy. Makes me want to bury my dick back inside you."

I roll my eyes, a small laugh escaping me. "I'm sure it does."

He kisses me then, a quick soft kiss. "Got to get back to work, baby," he says reluctantly. "I need you to do something for me when you leave."

I tilt my head back until my eyes meet his. "Anything."

Reaching into his pocket, he pulls out a scrap of paper. "Need you to go here and pick up a package for me. Bring it to me tomorrow at two o'clock, okay?"

"Okay."

He kisses me again, and then brushes his lips against the side of my neck, before letting me go. "I'll see you tomorrow, baby. Wait a couple minutes before you come out."

****

The drive to the address that Joshua gave me only takes a few minutes. I park in the driveway and stroll up to the door, knocking. It's late afternoon, the spring air warmer than normal.

The door opens and a man appears in front of me. He's older than me, perhaps mid-forties, with salt and pepper hair and beard. He stares at me, his expression blank, his eyes sliding over me before settling on my face.

The way he's looking at me sends a chill down my spine.

"Um, hi," I say, waving awkwardly. "Joshua sent me to pick something up."

He's silent for a beat, just staring, before he finally speaks. "You mean Swag?"

"Uh, yeah," I say, smiling bashfully. "Swag told me to come."

The man nods once, before disappearing back into the house, returning seconds later with a black duffle bag, handing it over. I take it, and go to say thank you, but I don't get the chance, the door closing before I can even open my mouth.

I blink a few times, staring at the closed door before turning around, hauling the duffle bag over to my truck. I toss it on the passenger's seat as I climb in, eyeing it, wondering what it is. Maybe it was the sex haze my brain was in when Joshua asked, but I never really thought about asking him what I was going to get.

But now that my head is clear, I'm realizing that whatever it is, it's not something he's supposed to have. If it were, it would be ordered and shipped to the prison.

Glaring at the back, I put my truck in drive, and back out of the driveway. It's not until I reach my apartment that my curiosity gets the better of me and I finally look inside.

25

This Call Is Being Recorded

———————

Have you ever woken up from a dream and felt unsettled, like that dream was trying to tell you something that you just really didn't want to know? And then there's that moment, the shattering moment when the sleepy fog clears and you realize that what you thought was a dream really wasn't a dream at all.

I've been stuck in that moment for what feels like days.

I'm on my back, lying in bed, staring up at the off-white popcorn ceiling. Becca is beside me, her hand twined in mine. She's been lying here with me since I opened that damn bag yesterday and had a little freak-out.

I should be happy right now. It's only been twenty-six hours since Joshua and I connected on a whole new level.

Shit. I should still be riding the wave of post-sex bliss, but I'm not.

Not even close.

That wave crashed into the shoreline like a goddamn tsunami the moment I opened that stupid bag.

It's fifteen minutes after four, and aside from the odd bathroom break, I haven't left my bed in a little under twenty-four hours.

My phone starts ringing again and my gaze goes back to it, back to his blinking name on the screen. I should answer it, I know I should, but it's been ringing non-stop for nearly ten minutes now, and I haven't been able to do it yet.

"You should answer it," Becca whispers, squeezing my hand. "If you don't do it soon, his guys are going to start showing up here."

"I know."

"Maybe if you just talk to him about it," she says, then hesitates. "Maybe there's a reason."

"Of course there's a reason," I say, when the phone quiets, then dings with another missed call notification. I shift my head, looking at her. "It's money. It has to be money. But couldn't he have just asked for money? He shouldn't have asked me to ..."

I let my words fall short and they hang in the air.

Becca gives me a sad smile. "Has he been asking you for money?"

"No. Never."

My phone starts ringing again, but I don't look at it, my gaze stuck on Becca's face. I can tell by her expression that she's not sure if she believes me, but it's the truth. Joshua Larson has never asked me for a single penny.

Never.

On the third ring, Becca lets go of my hand, popping up and reaching over me to grab my phone from the nightstand, and before I even realize what she's doing, she swipes the screen, putting the call on speaker.

"Becca, no," I protest, sitting up and reaching for the phone.

She holds it out of my reach, giving me a pointed look. "You're going to have to talk to him at some point. Might as well get it over with."

I flop back down on my bed, listening to the recording. The pause where his name is announced seems exaggerated, but when I finally hear the sound of his voice stating his name, a chill runs over my skin, twisting my stomach into knots.

The recording plays and plays, and when Becca has the chance to accept it, she does instantly. There's a long pause of silence that feels as though it lasts a whole freakin' day, before his anxious voice breaks through. "Are you okay?"

"I think so."

Silence.

"Then where the fuck were you today?"

There's a bite to his voice that makes me cringe. I glance at Becca, sitting beside me holding the phone, seeing the deep frown creasing her forehead. She opens her mouth, as though she's about to speak, but I quickly shake my head, quieting her.

I take a breath, and then, "I was at home. I, uh ..." I stall. "Becca's here with me and you're on speaker. I, uh ... I looked in the bag."

"Shit, baby, stop right there," he says. "This call is being recorded. You know we can't talk about this now."

Frowning, on the verge of tears from stress, I suck in a breath. "You asked. I'm just answering your damn question!"

"Watch your fucking tone," he says, his voice full of warning. He pauses for a beat, and I can hear him take a deep breath as though trying to calm himself. It doesn't work. "Come to a visit tonight."

"Jesus," Becca mutters. "You're an ass."

"Bitch, shut the fuck up," Joshua growls instantly. "This is between me and my woman. Keep your mouth shut or get the fuck out. You hear me?"

Silence.

I cut Becca a look, mouthing an *I'm sorry*. She merely shrugs, winks at me, and then flips off the screen before saying, "I hear you."

"Good," he says, then sighs. When he continues, his voice is softer. "Look, I've got to grab a shower, Victoria. Why don't you be here around five. We can talk then."

"I thought you were done with this shit," I say softly. "I thought you were—"

He lets out another sigh, cutting me off, but this time, it's long and gusty. "Baby, we can do this tonight *if* I decide I'm going to answer your questions."

I blink a few times. "If you decide?"

"Yes."

"What does that mean?"

"It means that there are certain things I'm just not going to talk to you about," he says. "That's it. Plain and simple."

I sit up straight, my eyes narrowing at the phone. "I moved out here for you, got a tattoo on my ass telling everyone I'm your property ... I think I have a right to know what's going on, especially if you're going to drag me into it."

"I'm done with this conversation."

"No, you're not done," I snap, anger and something that feels a hell of a lot like regret tinting my voice. "We need to talk about this. What am I supposed to do—"

"Enough," he growls, cutting me short. "I expect you to be here at five o'clock. We'll discuss this shit then, but just so you know, they could be recording us at the visit just like they're recording this phone call. So don't push—"

It's my turn to cut him off. "They don't record visits."

"Oh, they most certainly do. One of my lawyer's clients caught a Feds case because he said something at a visit. Do you want me to say the wrong thing and get more time in prison?"

I grit my teeth. "Of course not."

"Then you need to be mature about this and realize

that there's just some things I can't talk about," he says. "I expect you here at five."

Joshua doesn't give me a chance to respond, the recording telling me that he's already hung up. Becca laughs, shaking her head as she tosses the phone down and gets up. She goes straight to my closet, sliding the door open, and rooting around and calling out, "What do you want to wear?"

"I'm not going."

She pulls her head out of the closet and rolls her eyes. "Babe."

"I'm serious," I say, pulling the blankets up to my neck. "I'm not going. He can send someone to pick up his damn drugs, but I don't want to—"

"After everything you've been through with Richard, you're just going to throw it all away without even talking to him?" she asks, interrupting me. "Oh, no. No, that's not going to happen."

Her words take me back ten months to that first letter. To the excitement and the nerves. I was so happy when I received his first response. So giddy with joy.

How the hell did we go from excited and so lust-filled that we fucked in a restroom to this in twenty-four hours?

I just can't even wrap my head around it.

****

Forty-five minutes later, I'm sitting at table fourteen,

watching for Joshua to walk through the doors. I've got our drinks on the table, along with a bacon cheeseburger heated up waiting for him.

When I see him, the look on his face nearly knocks the wind out of me.

It's blank.

Completely and utterly blank.

I don't stand up when he approaches the table, too nervous to even try, and he doesn't ask me to, simply leaning down and placing a quick kiss on my cheek, before taking a seat across from me. He doesn't reach for his drink, doesn't even look at his burger. Instead, he folds his arms over his chest and just stares at me.

It's ... unnerving, that stare. So very different from the warm look he usually gives me. This look ... it chills me right down to the bones.

"You should eat," I say eventually, trying hard to hold his stare. It's a struggle. "It's going to get cold."

"I'm not hungry."

More silence.

Then, "Sometimes you're too nosey for your own good, you know that?"

"I told you I was nosey," I whisper, dropping my head because I can't stand another second of looking into those hard blank eyes. "You've always known that."

"You're right, I did," he says, matter-of-factly. "But it shouldn't matter. You say you love me, you say you'll do anything for me, and I ask you to do one fucking thing and you can't even do that for me. You're supposed to be my ol' lady, but you can't even do what you're fucking told."

"You asked me to pick up drugs," I whisper, my damn voice shaking. "You asked me to bring them—"

"I'm not talking about this here," he says abruptly, his tone hinting at the anger I can see brewing in his eyes. "They could be recording these tables."

"You're being paranoid."

"Maybe," he agrees. He leans forward then, plucking my hands off my knees and holding them tight, his touch sending tingles shooting through my body. "But maybe I'm not. How would you feel if you leave here and find out I got more time because you wouldn't let it go?"

I'd feel like an asshole. Even so ...

"How could you ask me to do that?"

"What do you want me to say?" he asks, the hard edge in his voice turning sharp. "That I thought you were down for me? That I fucking believed you when you said you'd do anything. Is that what you're looking for? You fucking knew who I was when you sent me that letter. You knew the kind of life I lived. And you fucking knew I've got no intention of leaving the club. I don't understand why you're making such a big thing out of this."

I look at him.

Really look at him.

And what I see there makes my entire body shake. The man I know is gone, replaced by the man who was able to pull the trigger.

"Who are you?" I whisper. I try to pull my hands away, but he holds on tight, his fingers wrapping around my wrist, keeping me still.

"Baby," he says. A quick flash of pain passes across his eyes, but it's gone in a blink, the anger burning bright once more. "This is my life. Always has been, and always fucking will."

But this isn't my life! I want to scream it at him and I want him to let go of my hands.

No. Scratch that. I need him to let go.

"Let go," I whisper. "I need to leave."

"You're not leaving," he says, his voice gritty with emotion. "You moved here for me. You've got my property tattoo on your ass. You're here to stay. You're not going anywhere. You belong to me."

"Let me go," I say again, this time a bit louder. "I'm serious, Joshua. Let me go or I swear I'll call one of the COs over here."

That grabs his attention. Slowly, he pulls his hands away, his hold on me loosening until it's gone altogether. I don't move. I can't. For a second I can't even breathe, too terrified of the man sitting before me, before I'm finally able to make my wobbly legs work, standing up.

"Baby," he says. He looks as though he's about to get to his feet, but he doesn't, his eyes darting over to the CO's desk, then back to me. "Don't do this, baby."

"I ... I ... I'm sorry," I whisper. "Please send someone to pick up your stuff."

And then, before I can change my mind, I turn and walk out the door. I make it to my car before the tears begin to streak down my face.

26

I Can't Quit You, Baby

———

Joshua hasn't called.

It's been nine days since I walked out on him and my phone hasn't rung once.

I don't know what to do about it.

I don't know if I want anything to be done about it.

My knight in shining armor turned out to be everything Richard told me he was: a criminal, a killer, a goddamn biker.

True, I knew all of that. Joshua never hid who he was from me, never really sugarcoated it, but as illogical as it is, I never thought I'd see it. Never thought my sheltered existence would cross paths with the darker side of his life.

I guess Richard was right on something else, too. I am naïve.

I spend the days alternating between hiding in my room and wandering around my new apartment, randomly unpacking a box here and there as I slip back into my normal routine of working too much.

I write.

I mope.

I call my parents and pretend everything's okay.

I stress.

And I judge.

It's the judgment that's killing me the most, I think. I don't like what it's doing to me. Don't like the way it's twisting me up and crushing my soul.

I don't want to be a cynical person.

But as it turns out, I am and I can't stop it.

I think about him constantly. I wonder how he's doing or how he's feeling. I can't get his voice out of my head. Can't get my body to stop craving his touch.

It's so goddamn lonely without him it makes my chest ache.

I wonder if he's thinking about me, too.

Obviously not.

Chow stopped by to pick up Joshua's stuff on day two, and I tried, oh God, did I try to find out how he was doing, if he was okay. I got nothing. I asked at least a million questions and every single one was met with stony silence.

He gave me absolutely nothing.

Not even a hint if Joshua was okay.

It was … frustrating. *Heartbreaking.*

Joshua came into my life when I needed him the most and he saved me. Saved me from myself. Saved me from the pain and the heartache I lived with daily.

He saved me from my life.

For the first time in years, I was happy and now ... it's gone.

He's gone.

I glance at my phone at least a hundred times a day, hoping that the thing will ring. But it doesn't. I wish I could call him, wish he had a goddamn phone, but he doesn't. So I just keep waiting for him to call me.

The sun rose hours ago, but the apartment is quiet. Becca's probably still sleeping, though I haven't ventured out of my room yet today to check. I should be sleeping, too. Inspiration hit the moment I got into bed last night, and I've been writing ever since.

I'm exhausted.

Glancing at my phone one last time, I save my work, and then close my laptop, setting it on the nightstand right beside my phone. I make sure the ringer is on, adjust and fluff my pillows, and then I lay back in bed, squeezing my eyes shut, hoping that maybe sleep will ease the ache in my chest. No sooner do I close my eyes and there's a knocking on my door. I glare at it, letting out an exaggerated sigh. "Come in."

Becca opens the door and walks in, her eyes fixed on the small box in her hands. "This just came for you. I think it's from—" She stalls, frowning as she glances up at me, her eyes widening when they land on me. "Jesus, Vickie, have you been up all night again?"

"Yup," I say, eyeing the box. "Who's it from?"

"Joshua's family, I think," she says, dropping down on the bed beside me. "The name on the return address just says Larson."

I sit up straight, blinking at her. My stomach flip-flops and I move to grab the box from her, but hesitate. "What is it?"

She rolls her eyes, laughing at me as she tosses it over, the box landing on my lap. "How the hell am I supposed to know?"

I stare at it.

The box is light and fairly small. It's the length of a letter-size envelope and maybe three inches in height. I read the return address, see the Larson name there, but I don't touch it.

I can't.

I'm too terrified of what the box might hold.

"Well," she says, nudging me with her elbow. "Aren't you going to open it?"

I swallow thickly, shaking my head. "I can't," I whisper. "I just ... can't. What if it's ..." I swallow again. "I don't want a goodbye."

And I really, truly don't. I know I'm the one that walked out, but ...

Becca laughs at me, rolling her eyes again. "Pretty sure goodbyes don't come by couriers."

Plucking the package off my lap, she grasps the easy-open strip and tears into it. Peeling the flaps back, she pulls out an envelope, glancing at it. "It says, 'Read me first.'" And then, without looking up at me, she opens it.

I'm instantly grateful for my best friend.

Becca doesn't look at the letter. She simply unfolds it, handing it over to me. And then, she waits.

May 21, 2016

Victoria,

I haven't heard from you for a week now and I must say it feels like a part of my heart is missing. I keep thinking that any day now you're going to show up at the prison, but you don't, and I'm starting to think that you never will.

I know that the conversation the last time we spoke shocked you or maybe showed you that I have a darker side to my life. I know you realized that I'm far from perfect, but it's our imperfections that make us who we are.

I need you to know that I'm sorry, beautiful. I thought trying to shelter you from my world was a mistake. Actually, I was scared you'd resent me for it, but I now realize trying to involve you was the mistake.

I've made a lot of mistakes in my life, but all of those mistakes lead me to you. Because of you, I've become a better man. You've showed me unconditional love and I'm afraid that my mistakes have ruined a lifetime of pure happiness we could have together.

Through your letters and kind words, I fell in love with you. The moment I laid eyes on you I knew you were the woman for me and when our lips touched, my heart melted.

From that moment on, I knew I wanted to marry you. You truly are perfect in my eyes, the woman of my dreams.

Please don't give up because you're scared of the unknown. All you need to know is that I'll love you until the day I die. I'll cherish every moment we share together. I'll forever hold you in my heart, a place only you can touch.

Victoria, I can't quit you, baby, so I hope you will give us a chance. Please, my beautiful angel, marry me.

All of my love now and forever,
Joshua

My hands are shaking.

I can't breathe.

I can't think.

"Vickie," Becca shouts, snapping her fingers in my face. "Vickie, are you listening to me?"

"No." My voice is a hoarse whisper and my eyes are burning. I lift a hand, scrubbing at them. It's then that I realize tears are streaking down my face. I blink up at Becca. "What did you say?"

"He sent you a ring," she screeches, shoving a small velvet box in my face. "Joshua sent you a ring."

I stare at the ring, taking the box from her and biting my bottom lip as I say, "He wants to marry me."

Becca pulls the note from my hand and I let it go without a fight, all my attention on the simple princess-cut diamond.

He wants to marry me.

Oh my God, he really wants to marry me.

As crazy as it is, I feel a bit better, because Joshua is still thinking about me.

He's not saying goodbye.

27

I've Been Waiting for You

When there's an impossible choice to make, when you must choose a path, how can you be sure you're making a choice that you won't regret?

Personally, I don't think you can be sure.

The only thing I know for certain: I love Joshua. I love him despite his flaws. When I strip everything away, all the judgment, all the fear and uncertainty, and I just look at him, at the man behind it all, I know I love him.

I stare down at the diamond sitting on my trembling finger. I've already gotten our drinks, and as always, his Swedish Fish are sitting on the table, waiting for him. I don't know what's going to happen, what he's going to think. I probably should have waited until he got here before getting the snacks, but the wait is taking too long and I needed to keep busy.

I glance at the clock again. It's been twenty-two minutes now.

Twenty-two minutes of sitting in this uncomfortable chair.

Twenty-two minutes of stressing and fidgeting.

I wonder if I should go ask about him. Maybe he's not even here. Maybe he's gotten into trouble and he's been put in segregation. Maybe he's …

The door opens, and I swing my head that way, my breath catching, then gushing out of me when I realize it's not him.

Another inmate walks in.

Another loved one stands up.

Another five minutes pass by.

I look to the CO's desk again. Five more minutes. I'll give it five more minutes and then …

The CO looks up then, glancing my way. He frowns at me, picking up the phone. I watch him for a moment, my brow furrowing as he hangs it up and walks over to me.

"I'm not sure what happened, ma'am," he says apologetically. "We called for him, but he didn't get the message."

"Oh, okay," I say, an equal mix of relief and nerves making my voice squeak. "Is he coming now?"

He nods, smiling warmly at me. "He should be here any minute."

"Thank you," I say, and he turns and strides away.

And then I wait.

And I watch.

And after a moment, the door opens, and Joshua steps through.

He doesn't look around, doesn't search me out like he always does. He steps up to the CO's desk, checking in, and it feels like a whole year passes before he finally looks my way.

He starts walking toward me then, and the look on his face has me sitting up straighter. It's a confusing look, one I've never seen before. It's relief. It's anger. It's fear. It's ... everything. A whole mish-mash of emotions wrapped all up into one beautifully terrifying look.

He stops beside me and I know he's waiting for me to get to my feet, but I don't stand up. I don't think my legs will hold me even if I try. They're wobbly and shaky, the damn things jiggle even when I'm sitting.

"Baby, why are you sitting down?" His voice is gruff, emotion making it thicker than normal.

"I don't know," I say, my voice sounding tiny and quiet in my ears. "I just ..."

Joshua grabs my hand before I can finish my sentence, yanking me up and pulling me to him, his arms wrapping around my body, his lips hitting mine before I can catch my breath. His fingers press into my flesh at the small of my back, pulling me tight against him. Then his tongue pries my lips open, darting into my mouth. His hand glides up my back, and he pulls my hair nice and hard.

I moan.

I can't help it.

I've missed his touch so much that the sound just pours out of me.

I completely forget where we are.

I try to get closer, need to get closer.

My body takes over, my fingernails digging into his neck, my crotch pressing against his thigh.

And then, he pulls away, murmuring against my lips, "I've been waiting for you."

He lets me go then, taking a seat at the table, and I can feel the heat rushing to my face as I glance around, spotting a few pairs of eyes looking our way.

It flusters me.

I scramble back to my chair and Joshua slouches back in his seat, watching me with a contented grin as I drop down—ungracefully. I have a million questions for him, a billion things I want to tell him, but all that comes out is, "I didn't know if I was ever going to come here again."

"I'm so glad you did, baby," he says. He scans me then, his eyes making a slow trail over my body, before settling on my hand. A slow grin splits his face. "You're wearing the ring I got you."

My eyes dart down to my hands, folded in my lap. I want to say something. I want to tell him I love it, that it's beautiful, but my voice betrays me when I try to speak.

My lips part, but the only thing that comes out is a gust of breath.

Joshua's grin turns into a wide smile and he holds out his hand to me. "Give me your hand, beautiful. Let me see it."

I do as he asks, silently extending my hand across the table, my fingers, my whole damn arm trembling. He takes it, his thumb rubbing up my ring finger, stalling when it brushes against the stone.

Silence falls.

He stares at the ring.

My stomach knots and my legs start to jump.

When he finally looks back up at me, there's a question in his eyes. "So I take it this means you're going to be my beautiful little wife?"

"Yes," I whisper. I don't mean to whisper it, but it seems as though my voice doesn't know that. I clear my throat, trying again. "Yes, I'll be your wife, um, if you still want me to be."

My response makes him laugh. "Baby girl, of course I still want you. I'm going to want you for the rest of my life."

"You didn't call," I point out. "You should have called."

"You left me," he says quietly, squeezing my hand within his. "I thought I lost you."

"I thought I lost you, too."

"Please don't ever scare me again like this," he says, his tone verging on pleading. "Don't care how mad you are or how scared you are, you still show up. You come to me. You talk to me. We deal with it together. You hear me?"

I nod. "I hear you."

He stares at me, searching my face as though he's trying to decide if he can trust me or not. I see it in his eyes the moment he realizes that I'm not going anywhere.

"I never stopped missing you," I tell him. "Never stopped thinking about you."

He doesn't respond right away, his gaze dropping to the ring for a moment, before he brings my hand to his lips, closing his eyes as he kisses the top. When his eyes open again, I see a softness there that I've never seen before. "You're mine forever."

"I'm yours," I whisper.

"Never forget it," he says. "Forever."

I nod, my eyes blurry with tears. "Forever."

Epilogue

Three years, two months, and ten days later.

Stepping through the gate, Joshua looks out across the parking lot toward me. The lot is packed today, and I'm stuck at the back.

I don't think he sees me.

I start toward him, lifting my hands over my head, waving to him. I know it the moment he spots me. His eyes zero in on me and a huge smile lights up his face, brighter than I've ever seen before.

It's beautiful.

It's freedom.

My heart stops, then races, and my legs just stop working. I want to run to him but the damn things won't move.

"Victoria Larson!" he calls out. "Get that sexy ass over here."

I laugh—hard—and shout back, "Who's Victoria Larson?"

He smirks and swaggers toward me, catching me by the back of my neck, pulling me into his body. "You," he says, and winks. "If you play your cards right."

I twine my arms around his neck. "Is that so?"

Lowering his head, pausing mere inches from my lips, he says, "Yeah, baby."

And then he kisses me.

His hands slide down my back until he reaches my ass. Grabbing handfuls, he hoists me up. Instinctively, my legs wrap around his waist.

He kisses me long and slow, a deep, meaningful kind of kiss that sends tremors running through me.

The tears come next. It's stupid, I know. I'd sworn I wouldn't cry. I'd promised myself that Joshua would not see a single tear from me today. But the damn things seep from my eyes anyway as his lips devour mine.

The last few years have been … rough. We've gone through a lot, Joshua and me. We've had our ups and our downs. There were times I wanted to give up. There were moments when not having him by my side was so hard I thought I'd go insane. But the moment our lips touch, the second I feel his tongue against mine, I realize that this moment right here, it's the moment I've been waiting for all my life, and suddenly, with crystal clear clarity, I know that if I could do it again, I wouldn't change a thing.

He breaks the kiss, looking down at me. "Why the tears, baby girl?"

I shrug helplessly. "Because I love you. Because I never thought this day would come. Because ... I just love you so freakin' much."

"Love you, too, beautiful," he says. "Always."

Joshua covers my mouth with his once more, kissing me softly, before sliding me back down to the ground, leaving me limp in his arms.

And then his hand is in my pocket, and he's digging around.

"What are you doing?" I ask, laughing because it tickles.

"Looking for the keys."

"Why?"

I balance awkwardly, sniffling and wiping away the tears, trying not to squirm too much as he grabs hold of them and yanks them free.

Grinning, he holds them up like they're some kind of trophy. "Because I need the keys if I'm going to drive."

I roll my eyes. "You're not driving my truck."

He doesn't reply, but his eyes say it all. There's no goddamn way I'm going to stop him. With a smirk, he turns and jogs over to my truck, climbing up behind the wheel.

Crap. He's serious. Eight years without being behind the wheel and he is going to drive my truck.

I stare at him, stunned, as he starts it up, rolling down the window. "Come on, Chipmunk. I need food. Good food. Real food. I fucking need steak."

I consider the situation. My truck is insured, I'm hungry, and steak is awesome.

"Okay," I say, jogging over to the truck and hopping up into the passenger seat. "Let's go get some steak."

Acknowledgements

A special thank you goes to Andrew. When I think about your unwavering support and encouragement, I can't help but feel grateful and blessed to have you in my life and on my side. Your enthusiasm is contagious, and I love you for it.

To my friends and family, thank you for sticking with me through another journey. Without your emotional support and feedback, *If I Could Do It Again* would still be stuck on the drawing board.

And to my editor, Kathryn, I couldn't have finished this book without you. You are a superstar and I'm so glad I have you on my team.

Last, but not least, a big thank you to all of my amazing readers. You all are the reason I keep writing. I love you all!

About the Author

Romance author Ashley Stoyanoff is the recipient of two Royal Dragonfly Book Awards for young adult and newbie fiction. Her first book, *The Soul's Mark: FOUND*, came out in 2012. Her other passions include reading and shopping for the latest fashions. Learn more about Ashley and her work at ashleystoyanoff.com.

8282789R00190

Printed in Germany
by Amazon Distribution
GmbH, Leipzig